WOL
Cumbria
County Council
Libraries, books and more.........
Cockermouth
1/22
MARYPORT
11/9/23
KT-491-523

Cumbria Libraries
CLIC
Interactive Catalogue

JOE O'BRIEN lives in Ballyfermot in Dublin with his wife and children. He is the author of the 'Danny Wilde' series – *Little Croker, Féile Fever* and *Tiger Boots* – about GAA player Danny and his friends, as well as *Beyond the Cherry Tree* and the 'Alfie Green' series for younger readers. His website is at www.joeobrienauthor.com

WHERE HISTORY IS MADE

THE O'BRIEN PRESS
DUBLIN

First published 2016 by
The O'Brien Press Ltd,
12 Terenure Road East, Rathgar,
Dublin 6, D06 HD27 Ireland.
Tel: +353 1 4923333; Fax: +353 1 4922777
E-mail: books@obrien.ie.
Website: www.obrien.ie

ISBN: 978-1-84717-826-8

7 6 5 4 3 2 1
20 19 18 17 16

Printed and bound by Norhaven Paperback A/S, Denmark.
The paper in this book is produced using pulp from managed forests

DEDICATION

For all the football friends I have had the privilege to share the beautiful game with.
You're all LEGENDS!

ACKNOWLEDGEMENTS

A huge thanks to Michael, Ivan and all the team at The O'Brien Press, especially my editor Helen Carr, Emma Byrne for the fantastic cover design, and Ruth, Geraldine, Brenda and Sarah for all the help with promotion and sales.

A big thank you as always to all the booksellers, librarians and everyone dedicated to the world of children's books, for the support and enthusiasm that plays a huge part in writer's books reaching the hands of readers.

Thank you to all my readers. You are the reason I write.

I would like to thank my two favourite footballers, Jamie and Tamzin, for all their smiles, hugs and unconditional love and support to me as a dad and a writer.

Finally, I would like to thank my wife and best friend, Mandy, for her unrivalled support and encouragement.

AUTHOR'S NOTE

One of the greatest footballers of all time, Pele, once described football as 'The Beautiful Game'. I started playing the beautiful game at a very young age and to this day I still enjoy kicking a ball around with some of the friends I made when I was a young boy. As a token of appreciation of our life-long friendship, I have named some of the characters in the book after them.

Football is not just about kicking a ball. It's about friendship, being part of a team, helping others both on and off the playing field, respecting oneself and others too, building confidence and challenging oneself to new goals, but most of all football is about enjoyment and having fun.

I hope you find all of these attributes in my book and enjoy reading *Legends' Lair* as much as I enjoyed writing it.

Joe O'Brien

CONTENTS

CHAPTER 1

ON THE VOLLEY

Charlie Stubbs had one passion in life – *football.* Charlie cared about football more than anything else in the world. Everywhere he went, he took his ball with him – after all, what was the point in going somewhere if you couldn't kick a ball when you got there?

Luckily for Charlie, his dad felt the same way. Charlie and his dad couldn't be closer; they were so tight that Charlie's mum called them the *Super Glue Two.*

Charlie's dad always met him at the school gates every Friday. It was their special thing. They would drop into the park on the way home for a kick about, before picking up a fish and chippy.

'Pass it, Da!' Charlie called out as he ran toward the goal.

SWISH

Charlie's dad swung a beautiful ball into the box.

SMACK

Charlie caught the ball on the volley with his right foot and clattered it off the left post, into the goal.

'Goooooooooal!' Charlie celebrated. He ran around in a circle and then dived into a slide, eventually rolling over on his back, staring up at the sky.

Charlie's dad was in stitches. 'You're a spacer, son, d'you know that?'

Charlie's dad lay down beside his son and they both breathed in the smell of the freshly cut grass and stared up at the clouds passing over, each letting their own thoughts come into their heads and then drift away into the calm blue sky.

It was certain that the two were thinking about the same thing – football. Charlie was thinking how great it would be if he scored a volley just as good in his match tomorrow against Broughton United in the last game of the season.

His dad was thinking how great it would be if he somehow, magically, found his way into Old Trafford Stadium on Sunday.

Charlie rolled his head over to one side and smiled at his dad.

'I got it from you, Da.'

'Got what from me?' his dad asked.

'It must be in the genes.'

'You've lost me, son.' Charlie's dad was confused.

'You said I was a spacer. I got it from you!' chuckled Charlie. 'It must be in the genes.'

Charlie's dad laughed. 'You can't go wrong so, son. I only wear the best of jeans.'

Charlie pushed his dad and the two began to wrestle.

That's the way Charlie and his dad were. They were more than just father and son. They were pals – best pals.

Charlie was an only child. He was born in Dublin, where his mum and dad were from, but six years ago, when Charlie was six, they moved to Salford, in England, just three miles north of Old Trafford in Manchester.

The move was very tough on Charlie. He had great friends and family back in Dublin, and starting all over in a new city and a new country was a monumental task.

But there was one big bonus that came with the move; Old Trafford was just three miles away and Charlie and his dad were Manchester United fans.

'Big game on Sunday, Da,' said Charlie, sitting back up.

'I wish we could go, son,' said Charlie's dad.

'I know. United v City – home derby. It's gonna be classic.'

'What score d'you think it'll be, son?'

'Three nil United, Da.'

'I hope so, son,' smiled Charlie's dad. 'Are you excited about your match tomorrow?'

'I'm mad for it. We can't win the league, but if we beat Broughton we can finish second.' Charlie jumped up and ran over to his ball. 'Come on, Da. Hop in goal and I'll have a few shots on ya!'

Charlie's dad was a bit slow getting to his feet.

'You all right, Da?'

'I'm grand, son – brand new!' smiled Charlie's dad. 'Just got a bit dizzy there. Tell you what – one of the lads in work was telling me the other day about some Brazilian fella who holds the Guinness world record for keepy-uppies.'

Charlie's eyes lit up. 'How many?'

'Fifteen thousand, I think he said.'

'What? No way! *Fifteen thousand*?' Charlie gasped. 'He must have been at it for weeks.'

Charlie's dad shook his head. 'I'm sure he said he did it in two hours or something like that.'

'Two hours. Who was he? Was it Neymar? Was it Oscar? He's deadly at doing tricks.'

Charlie's dad shook his head again. 'No, he wasn't a professional. He was just some fella from Brazil. You know what they're like in Brazil. They play football in their sleep.'

'Have you got your watch?' Charlie clipped the ball up between his two feet and started doing keepy-uppies.

'Go on,' smiled his dad. 'But we haven't got two hours. Your mammy will be looking for her chippy so you'll have to keep it going as we're walking.' Just then his phone rang. He glanced at the screen and smiled at Charlie, who was switching the ball back and forth from left to right foot. 'Speak of the devil,' laughed Charlie's dad. 'How are you, love? We won't be long ...'

Charlie was counting his keepy-uppies while his dad spoke to his mum.

'Forty-three, forty-four, forty-five …'

'Okay, love. We're on the move. See you shortly – bye.' Charlie's dad slipped his phone back into his pocket. 'Right, son, we're off.'

'Fifty-nine – sixty. I'm counting, Da!'

'Come on, Charlie. Mammy got a call from your gran. Their plane lands at seven and we've got to pick them up from the airport.'

'We've loads of time. Seventy-one, seventy-two.' Charlie flicked the ball up into the air and began to head it. 'Seventy-seven, seventy-eight …'

Charlie's dad was impressed. He knew Charlie was a class player, but he was dazzled by Charlie's overall control of a football. Charlie was what was known in football as a complete player: somebody who had it all – the whole game.

That's why a scout from Manchester United had been keeping a close eye on Charlie all season, and this made his dad very proud. Whatever doubts he had when they first moved to Salford about doing the right thing had diminished. Charlie was happy now, that's all that mattered to his dad and as he watched his son control the ball as if he was dancing with the one love of his life, Charlie's dad's heart swelled with happiness.

'Ninety-two … All right, Da! I'm coming then. Get in goal and I'll have one last shot on ya.'

Charlie's dad stood tall and large in the goal mouth. Charlie had it all worked out. He'd drop the ball back down to his feet when he got to ninety-nine and then he'd let it rip.

'Ninety-six, ninety-seven …'

Charlie took a swift glance at the goal. He picked his spot. He dropped the ball down to his left knee on ninety-eight and then to his left foot on ninety-nine.

'A HUNDRED!!!' yelled Charlie as he switched the ball over to his right foot and swung at it.

THUMP

Charlie caught the ball nice and sweet on the volley and lashed it toward the goal.

Just as the ball reached his dad and he stretched out his hands, the ball swerved to the right and shot through the top right corner of the goal.

'Can I get a drink in the chippy, Da?' asked Charlie, as cool as a cucumber. 'I'm gaggin'.'

CHAPTER 2

HALF TIME

Twenty-two minutes past seven, the doors of Arrivals at Manchester airport slid open and Charlie's grandparents and his Uncle Tony walked through. Charlie waved his hands to catch their attention. He hadn't seen them since Christmas, when he was in Dublin for a few nights. Everybody hugged and seemed very happy to see each other again, but Charlie noticed that there was something not right between his dad and his Granddad.

Charlie remembered walking into his granddad's kitchen in Dublin and finding them having an argument.

I thought they'd sorted that? Charlie thought. *Dad said it was nothing.*

Things didn't improve on the way home in the car. Charlie tried his best to get his dad and his granddad talking, but the most he got was a 'yes' or a 'no' or sometimes he barely got a murmur.

Uncle Tony did his best to keep the spirits up. He began to tell Charlie stories of when he and Charlie's dad were small and the things they got up to. Uncle Tony was the younger brother by two years; it was Charlie's dad's fortieth birthday and that's why they were visiting. There would be a party in the local pub tomorrow night.

Later that night, Charlie's dad and Uncle Tony went down to the local pub for a couple of pints to catch up. They had asked Granddad to join them, but he said that he was too tired from travelling.

Charlie saw this as an opportunity to have a chat with his granddad. He didn't like the atmosphere between two people that he loved so dearly and he knew that both of them were suffering.

I'll see if I can get Granddad to cheer up and be friends with dad again, Charlie thought.

Granddad was out the back garden having a sneaky smoke. He'd given up smoking years ago, but he always kept one or two in a packet for emergencies, usually if he was worried about something or he was feeling stressed.

Charlie sat up on the fence that Granddad was leaning against.

'You caught me!' smiled Granddad.

'You know them things are bad for ya, don't you, Granddad?'

Granddad chuckled and then he coughed. 'They are!' Granddad winked. 'But don't tell your gran, or this ciggy will be the least of my worries.'

'Em, Granddad, can I ask you a question?' Charlie asked.

'You just did!' smiled his granddad.

'Nice one!' giggled Charlie. He knew this wasn't going to be easy, but he was determined to get to the bottom of whatever was driving a wedge between his granddad and his dad.

'Why didn't you go out with Da and Uncle Tony?'

Granddad sucked in a big mouthful of smoke and as he exhaled, Charlie could almost feel the tension in the air.

Granddad looked at Charlie. 'I'm jaded, Charlie.'

There was silence for a moment or two. Charlie wasn't sure how to approach things, after thinking about it he figured that the only way he was going to get the truth from Granddad was to ask him out straight.

'So you and Da aren't talking. What's that all about then?'

Granddad pressed his cigarette against the fence to put it out. Charlie could see that his hand was trembling.

Charlie reached over and put his arm around his granddad's shoulder.

'You all right, Granddad? You have me worried for ya.'

Granddad patted Charlie on the back. 'I'm fine, kid.'

'You haven't answered my question!'

'You ask a lot of questions for a youngster.' Charlie raised both eyebrows as if to say, *I'm still waiting!* 'Ah, you know, sometimes Charlie, people who love each other very much, have different opinions and well, sometimes they just don't agree on things and well, you know …' Granddad was finding it difficult to answer Charlie's question.

'Is it to do with the fight you and Da had back in Dublin?' Charlie asked.

Granddad blushed. 'I'm sorry, Charlie, that you saw us arguing. You should never have seen that.'

'Relax, Granddad' said Charlie. 'It's no big deal. People argue all the time. This one time, me and another fella off the team had a big scrap on the pitch. We're both centre-mids and we weren't getting on for a while. It was over something really stupid in training; an argument. We were fairly good pals up to that, not best friends like or anything like that, but we got on all right. Anyway, we were both taken off by the manager and didn't play for the rest of the game. We lost that match. Thinking back now, if we hadn't been fighting I know we would have won that game. We were both unhappy and everyone on the team was unhappy so we shook hands at the next training session and got on with it.' Charlie tapped his granddad on the arm. 'Sometimes, Granddad, if you want to be happy again, and everyone around you too, you have to just get over it and get on with it.'

A big smile beamed across his granddad's face; Charlie could see all the stress and anguish lift.

'Come here, you, and give this foolish old man a hug,' said Granddad.

Charlie could feel granddad's heart beating against his chest. He loved his granddad to pieces and his daddy too.

HALF TIME, Charlie thought. *Need to speak to dad to get FULL TIME on this problem.*

CHAPTER 3

MATCH DAY

Match day and Charlie was out of bed at the crack of dawn as they were every Saturday morning during football season. His grandparents were in the kitchen with his mum, making a big Irish breakfast.

'Aw, that smells delicious,' Charlie licked his lips as he strolled into the kitchen.

'How are you, pet?' asked Charlie's gran. 'Come and give your gran a big hug.'

Charlie threw his arms around her. It didn't bother Charlie to show affection. He had grown up in a loving environment and was never embarrassed to dish out the hugs.

'All right, Granddad?' Charlie winked.

Granddad winked back.

'What are you two up to?' smiled Charlie's mum.

'Nothing, Mam. Dad not up yet?'

'He's in bed, the lazy sod,' said his gran.

'Couple of beers too many,' smiled Granddad.

'Not for much longer!' laughed Charlie. 'No lay-ins on match day.'

Charlie ran upstairs, grabbed a hold of his dad's bed covers and with one big *SWISH* he blasted a draft right up under the duvet.

'Oh my head!' groaned Charlie's dad.

Charlie dived onto the bed. 'Come on you – up for the match.'

Charlie's dad turned over, both hands to his head. 'What time is it?'

'Quarter to eight,' said Charlie.

'What time is your match?'

'It's at half ten, but we're meeting at the pitch at half nine.'

Charlie's dad sat up and pulled the covers up to his chin. 'Half nine, son? That's an hour before the match.'

Charlie nodded. 'I know, but Andy wants to run through a few things with us before the game – it's the last game of the season and runner-up position is up for grabs.'

Charlie's dad smiled and shook his head. 'All right then, I'm up, son. I'll jump in the shower.'

Charlie remembered that he wanted to have a chat with his dad, about Granddad.

'Em! Da, I need to have a chat with ya.'

'Is it important?' his dad asked.

'Very.'

'Can I have my shower first?'

'Sound,' smiled Charlie. 'Sure, look, it can wait 'til later. I need to get me head in match mode, all right?'

'Bang on, son,' his dad winked. 'Do me a favour though, will ya?'

Charlie jumped up off the bed.

'What?'

Charlie's dad had a big grin on his face. 'Go in and jump on your Uncle Tony. He's in a worse state than me.'

Father and son laughed together. That sounded like a good plan.

* * *

Charlie's team were called the Salford Devils. They were in the City of Salford League under 12's division 1. It was the last game of the season and the Devils were playing league leaders, Broughton United at home.

Broughton had already won the league. They were five points clear at the top and couldn't be overtaken. Charlie's team were in second place, just one point ahead of third place, Beechfield Aces.

The Devils needed a win to secure runner-up position. A draw or a defeat could mean losing that spot to the Aces if they won their match on the far side of Salford.

Andy, the Devils' manager, had set up a few grids with his assistant, Phil. They weren't training grids, just warm-up grids to make sure that their players were on their toes and fresh for the crucial match.

'Will I call them over?' Phil asked Andy.

Andy looked at his watch. 'Give 'em a few more minutes, Phil.

Look who's over there. I wanna go over and have a chat with him.'

Andy was referring to a scout from United; the one who had been keeping a close eye on Charlie for most of the season.

The team were scattered around the pitch. Some were kicking a ball to each other. Some were having shots on the goal and the rest were hanging around the sideline chatting.

Charlie was at the top end of the pitch with his dad and his Uncle Tony. Charlie always had a few minutes with his dad, away from the team, before they were all called together. Charlie knew that his dad had been a great footballer when he was younger and Charlie buzzed off that. He loved the little bits of advice his dad would give him before each game; he had a special way of lifting his son's spirit and confidence before every game – the odd few words of wisdom in an encouraging way.

Charlie loved that. It was a special bond he had with his father.

'Hey! Uncle Tony!' Charlie called. 'Hop in goal with Da and I'll have a shot on the two of yiz.'

Uncle Tony stood beside Charlie's dad in the goal mouth.

Charlie's dad nudged his brother. 'Move over a bit, you big lump.'

'Relax,' smiled Tony. 'He'll never get it past the two of us.'

Charlie's dad smiled at Tony, 'Don't let him hear you saying that.'

Suddenly, Phil blew hard on his whistle. Charlie looked around and saw his teammates sprint over to their coach.

'Come on, kid!' smiled Tony.

Charlie turned back and focused on the goal. He picked his

spot. That's where he would put the ball. He wouldn't ever change his mind once he had his spot picked. That's one of the things his dad taught him.

SWISH!

Charlie swerved the ball around Tony's right ear, into the top left corner of the net.

'Catch yiz in a while!' Charlie waved and ran over to join his team mates.

Tony stood still, his hands in the same position as they were before Charlie took his shot. He turned to his brother, who had a huge grin on his face.

'I told you!' laughed Charlie's dad.

'Jaysis!' gasped Tony. 'I didn't even get a chance to move. He's a class act.'

Charlie's dad nodded, pride beaming from his face.

'D'you see your man over there, talking to Charlie's manager.'

'Yeah,' Tony nodded.

'He's the scout from United, I was telling you about.'

'He's here to watch Charlie?'

'I'd say so,' said Charlie's dad. 'Fingers crossed, please God.'

CHAPTER 4

DEVILS V BROUGHTON

Broughton had turned up early for the game. They also ran through a few warm-up grids before kick-off, and even though they had already won the league, they were playing for pride. They didn't want to lose their last game of the season.

The referee had already checked the players' boots and had his few words with them; nothing serious, just a bit of advice on how to play fair and no dirty tackles.

'Always listen for the whistle,' the ref said, 'and if there's any bad-mouthing from the sidelines, don't worry about it. I'll sort that out.'

Andy had his team named and their positions picked – the keeper, with a three-three-two formation.

Charlie was starting in centre-mid, his usual position and he was wearing his lucky number seven. Charlie was without any doubt, the best player on his team – the most skilful and as Andy would say, '*Charlie 'ad the 'head of a pro on 'im!'*

Charlie was named captain for the final match. It had nothing to do with favouritism or even the fact that he was the best player on the team. Everyone on the team had a chance to be captain and today it was Charlie's turn.

'Are yiz up for it, lads?' The ref smiled at the two captains in the centre circle. Both players nodded. 'We'll have a handshake, so,' the ref nodded.

Charlie stretched out his right hand and was met by a tight grasp from the Broughton number eight.

'I want a fair game then, and lots of encouragement and good leadership from you lads,' said the ref as he handed the match ball to Charlie.

'All right, lad. Let's be 'aving ya, so.'

Charlie dropped the ball to the ground as the ref waved the Broughton captain and his fellow midfielder back from the centre spot.

Charlie glanced back to see if his team were in proper shape. He nodded to his goal keeper and then he quickly glanced over to the sidelines – one nod for his coaches and a smile to his dad and Uncle Tony.

Once Charlie returned his eyes back to the ball, there was only one thing in his thoughts as he stared down the Broughton captain, *Yiz beat us already, but you'll not be having three points today!*

The ref blew his whistle and Charlie tapped the ball to his number ten, who passed it back to the Devils' centre half.

The match had begun – the final contest of the season to be

played on the Salford Park small-sided pitch.

The Devils' centre half knocked the ball out towards their right mid, but he kicked it too hard. It was a throw in for Broughton.

Charlie sensed nervousness in his team. This was an important game and there was a lot to play for.

'Settle down, Tom,' Charlie waved over to his centre half. 'Relax – time on the ball.'

That's what Andy, his coach meant when he'd said that Charlie had the head of a pro. Charlie could read a game better than most in his age group. In fact, Charlie could read the game better than most – period!

The Broughton full back threw the ball up the line and sent his left mid running at the Devils' right back. The Broughton number six showed blitzing pace as he flew past the Devils' number two and knocked a cracking ball into the box to one of his forwards who caught it on the bounce and struck it sweetly past the Devils' keeper and into the back of the net.

GOAL!

Everyone on the Broughton line jumped and cheered.

Charlie glanced over to the sideline. He noticed Andy had his hands to his face. It was a disastrous start.

Charlie switched his eyes toward his dad who just put both thumbs up and then clapped his hands, 'Come on the Devils,' he yelled. 'Let's get it going.'

Charlie's granddad had arrived and was standing next to Uncle Tony. He was clapping his hands too and he gave Charlie a wave of encouragement.

Charlie nodded over and raised his head. He then repeated exactly what his dad had cheered. It was infectious. Suddenly everyone along the Devils' sideline was chanting the same.

Even Andy was waving his team on.

As Charlie approached the centre spot, he turned around and called in his centre half and left mid. Charlie kept his voice down and put his hands to his mouth to muffle his words so the Broughton midfielders couldn't make out what he was saying.

'As soon as the ball comes back to you,' Charlie said to his centre half, 'hold it up for a few seconds and give me a chance to get forward.' Charlie looked to his left mid, who wore number six. 'Then pass it to Harvey.'

'Then what?' Harvey asked.

'I'll move into a space in front of their centre half. You'll see me pointing to the ground. Just knock it to me. I'll do the rest.'

Charlie's team mates nodded. The plan was set. All they had to do was get the ball to Charlie. That meant two pinpoint passes, with no room for error.

The ref gave Charlie a nod and Charlie tipped off. His number ten once again passed the ball back to the Devils' centre half who took a touch and held it just long enough for the Devils' left mid to move into a space to the left of his marker.

As the Broughton forwards ran toward the Devils' centre half, he took a quick look then hit a long and accurate pass along the ground to his left mid.

Charlie had already run into position. He'd left the Broughton midfielders in midfield, and he'd moved into a space in front of the Broughton centre half, as planned.

The Devils' left mid ran with the ball and just as one of the Broughton full backs came in for a tackle, he side stepped him and took a look for Charlie.

Charlie was pointing to his right. That was the signal – that's where Charlie wanted the ball.

As Charlie made his move, his left mid passed the ball to him and Charlie took one touch and back flicked it around the Broughton centre half who had ran with him.

Charlie spun around the centre half, leaving him dazed.

'Go on, Charlie!' came cheers from the Devils' sideline.

Charlie was through. He raced toward goal with the ball stuck to his right boot.

The Broughton left back ran in toward Charlie to put in a tackle but Charlie pulled off a double step over and skilled him.

Now, there was only the Broughton keeper to beat who wasn't sure whether to come off his line or not.

Charlie took one final glance at goal. *I'll smash it!* he thought.

But just as the Broughton keeper came out and Charlie was about to strike the ball, he noticed that the Broughton right back had kept one of the Devils' forwards onside. Charlie unselfishly switched the ball across to his number 11 who had ran toward goal.

The Devils' forward beat his marker to the ball and side footed it past the Broughton keeper into the net.

GOAL!

One all! Everyone on the Devils' sideline was ecstatic.

'That was special!' Charlie's dad over heard a parent beside him. He looked over toward the United scout who had his eyes fixed upon Charlie. *Charlie couldn't have picked a better game to pull a move like that,* his dad thought.

The game tightened up after that piece of magic from Charlie and his team mates. Broughton were under strict instruction from their sideline to mark tighter.

As the referee blew the half-time whistle, the game stood at one all and all the players ran over to their coaches, parched and tired.

Phil opened up a bag of freshly cut oranges.

'Dive in, lads!' said Pill. 'It's scorching. They'll do yiz no harm, eh?'

As every single player sucked on their oranges, Andy delivered his half time talk.

It was short and it was sweet – just a commendation on their hard work and good passing. It was never going to be an easy task keeping Broughton at bay, but the Devils were doing just that and Andy knew the longer the game went on at one all, the more frustrated Broughton would become.

'I'm going to make a couple of changes lads, okay?' said Andy, just before the referee gave the signal for the second half.

The Devils' coach made three changes, the right back – one of the forwards and he put his hand on Charlie's shoulder. 'I'm taking you off for a breather, kid.'

Charlie didn't mind. He knew the score. Everyone had to have a chance to play and he was a team player, so if that's what the coach wanted then Charlie went along with it – no complaints.

Broughton tipped off the second half with a vengeance. Whatever their coach had said to them at half time was working as they pounded the Devils' half of the pitch from the word go.

Charlie was chewing his fingers watching from the sideline as his team struggled against a much stronger Broughton than the first half. But Andy hadn't intended on leaving Charlie on the line for long. He knew that the United scout was at the match to watch Charlie play and he wasn't going to ruin his chances by leaving him off.

Ten minutes in and Broughton had a corner. Andy signalled the referee and called the Devils' left mid off.

'Go on, kid,' Andy looked at Charlie. 'Slot in there.'

Charlie gave his dad and Uncle Tony a nod before running on.

'COME ON THE DEVILS!!' Charlie heard his dad roar. That cheer sent an electric spark through Charlie as he raced over to the Devils' goalmouth to mark a Broughton player.

The Broughton number seven swung a beautiful and dangerous corner into the box. The ball flew pass three players and found its way to one of the Broughton midfielders who swung his left boot at it.

Just as he connected with the ball, Charlie stretched out his left leg and blocked it down, sending the ball away to the left side of the pitch where the Devils' left back raced to collect it and knock it up to one of his forwards.

Charlie had displayed just how good a player he was defensively as well as technically.

That really lifted the Devils' spirits, and brought them right back into the game. There was nothing between the two sides for the last ten minutes.

Just as the Devils were on the attack for what looked like the last move of the match, their right mid was hacked down just outside the Broughton box.

The ref blew hard on his whistle and immediately reached for a yellow card.

Andy and Phil ran onto the pitch to see if their player was okay. After a few minutes he managed to get to his feet, but he had to come off.

As Phil was walking off the pitch, Charlie heard him asking the referee something.

'Could be one of the last kicks of the game! Not long left,' the referee answered.

Charlie looked over toward Andy who gave him a signal to take the free kick.

Charlie rolled the ball under his right foot as the referee moved the Broughton wall back.

This is it! Charlie thought. *Last kick of the season – we need the win to be sure.*

As both teams struggled in the box, Charlie only had one

thought in his head and that was to put the ball in the Broughton net.

'When you're ready, kid,' nodded the ref.

All the Salford Devils supporters were up at the far end of the line, right in line with Charlie and the Broughton goal.

Just as Charlie stepped back to take the free, he noticed his number ten signalling to him. It was a signal for something they had practised in training.

Charlie knew the referee was ready to blow the game up, but would it be possible? Would he allow the time?

The wall was an obstruction – Charlie knew this.

Okay then! Charlie nodded, as he passed the ball to the feet of his forward. The wall suddenly broke up and she rolled the ball back into the path of Charlie. The Salford Devils' captain leaned back and CURLED it around the two Broughton players who were the remains of the wall.

GOAL!

The referee blew his whistle. FULL TIME!

They'd done it.

Charlie went on a solo toward the Devils' sideline, followed by all his team mates.

The Devils supporters were hysterical. What a way to clinch runner-up in the league and to do it against the league winners on home turf!

Andy and Phil were quick to line all the players up in the centre of the pitch to shake hands. That was something that all teams did after a match. Win or lose, the handshake was the seal of respect to your opponent and the game of football regardless of the result or what went on during the match.

As soon as the handshake was over, Charlie headed toward his family.

Charlie's dad wrapped his right arm around his son. 'Well done, kid, proud of ya.'

Granddad and Uncle Tony were next to congratulate Charlie.

'You'll be playing in Old Trafford next season Charlie, after that performance!' said Tony as he patted Charlie on the arm.

Charlie was beaming with pride.

'Now don't let the head swell too much,' smiled Granddad. 'But if I must say, you were very good out there, lad. You've a cracking little team there. It's a shame you're not playing for your oul granddad's club, back home in Dublin.'

Even though Granddad was only kidding, Charlie's dad almost snapped his head off, 'Will you leave it out?'

'Dad!' said Charlie.

'You always have to have your say, don't ya? Sure what does it matter where he plays as long as he's happy. We're happy here in Salford and we've no plans to go home – ALL RIGHT?'

'I'm only joking,' chuckled Granddad. 'Don't be getting your head in a twist.' And he turned to walk away.

Charlie was gutted. He'd been so happy just a minute ago and now his dad and Granddad were fighting again.

Just as I thought I could bring them close again! Charlie thought.

Uncle Tony raised his eyebrows toward Charlie's dad as if to say, *There was no need for that.*

'Sorry, Charlie,' his dad apologised.

'I'll go after him,' said Uncle Tony. 'Charlie, your coach and your man from United are heading over to yiz, so chin up.'

Charlie's coach introduced the scout from United to Charlie and his dad.

'Very impressive performance out there, Charlie' said the United scout. 'Capped off a great season for you.'

'Thanks,' smiled Charlie. He was trying to look calm and confident, but inside he was a nervous wreck, worrying if he had done enough to convince the scout that he had what it takes to make it to the top.

The scout didn't delay in putting Charlie out of his misery.

'We'd love to have you over at the training grounds with us, if you're up for that? What d'you think, lad?'

Charlie looked at his dad and released a big breath of relief.

Charlie's dad nodded to Charlie as if to say, *Go on then, answer the man.*

'Mint!' gasped Charlie. 'Yeah! Yeah – big time!'

The scout laughed and then turned to Charlie's coach. 'Super – I'll get the ball rolling then and give you a call.'

Andy shook the scout's hand and then Charlie's dad lunged his hand out too, followed by Charlie.

As Charlie's coach walked off with the scout, he looked back and winked a *Well done, lad*, to Charlie.

Charlie's dad playfully pushed him over, 'Come on Super Star, and we'll get home and tell your mammy you'll be taking orders from Old Trafford from now on.'

Charlie was buzzing. He felt like he was about to explode with happiness.

United! thought Charlie as he walked off the pitch with his dad. *This is just the beginning!*

CHAPTER 5

THEATRE OF DREAMS

There was a double celebration in the Salford Arms that night. Charlie's dad was adamant that everybody at his birthday party would hear about Charlie's trial with United. And to top off a brilliant night, Charlie's dad got the best present he could have wished for. Charlie had kept it secret for weeks. He knew that his dad would have loved to go and watch the home derby against City, and when Charlie heard of two tickets up for grabs, he persuaded his mum to go halves with him and treat his dad.

Of course, as there were two tickets, Charlie would get to go and watch his first ever derby match.

* * *

As the crowd gathered along Sir Matt Busby Way, Charlie and his dad joined in with the chants outside the Theatre of Dreams.

UNITED! UNITED! UNITED!

Charlie had just bought a new scarf from one of the stalls and he ran over to stand under *THE UNITED TRINITY* bronze statues of Best, Law and Charlton, three of the best and most gifted United players of all time.

'Come on, Da!' waved Charlie. 'Get your phone out and take a picture.'

Charlie's dad laughed. 'You must have a dozen of pictures under the Trinity, son.'

'Not with me new scarf, Da, come on?' Charlie raised his scarf over his head, pride beaming from his face.

His mind began to drift, dreaming that maybe one day, a bronze statue of Charlie Stubbs would be erected outside the Theatre of Dreams, just like Bobby Charlton, the greatest football genius of them all. Charlie thought of everything Charlton had achieved in football, from winning the world cup in 1966 to scoring two goals for Man United in the 1968 European Cup final and even winning the Ballon d'Or award in 1966 for football player of the year.

As Charlie snapped out of his thoughts to his dad's voice, he glanced back and winked at the statue of Sir Bobby Charlton, who came up with the nickname for Old Trafford.

Even though Charlie and his dad were early, the stadium was already filling up. Father and son took their seats in The Sir Alex Ferguson North Stand facing the dugouts in the Sir Bobby Charlton South Stand. The Man City fans were chanting at the top of their voices from down in the South East Stand.

'Cover your ears, son,' Charlie's dad smiled.

'They won't be singing that, Da, when we put the ball in the back of their net.'

* * *

The match started slow and was dirty and riddled with tension. City had already picked up a couple of yellow cards for badly timed tackles in the first ten minutes. But the atmosphere as always in Old Trafford was buzzing. Charlie was munching his bag of crisps when United surged forward down the left wing chasing a long pass from defense.

'Go on!' shouted Charlie. 'Knock it into the box.'

Just as Charlie had cried out, the ball swung beautifully across the box. The City keeper was slow to come off his line. Charlie's heart skipped a couple of beats.

BANG!

GOAL ......

'Screamer!!' cheered Charlie. His bag of crisps scattered into the air like confetti.

Charlie and his dad danced and sang along with the rest of the United army as the keeper picked the ball out of the back of his net and thumped it up the pitch.

You could hear a pin drop in the South East stand. All the City fans were devastated.

That was to be the only goal in the match. It wasn't the greatest game of football, but United had come out of it with three points and Charlie was thrilled that his team – and more importantly, his dad's team – had won on his dad's birthday, and they were both there, in the Theatre of Dreams. It was a day neither of them would ever forget.

On the way home, Charlie got it into his head that he still wanted to have his chat with his dad about Granddad. It was about a three-mile walk home and Charlie's dad was in top form.

I think now is as good a time as ever! Charlie thought as they walked through the gates of Salford Park.

'I wish I had me ball, Da,' smiled Charlie as they passed the football pitches.

'You're a gas man,' laughed his dad. 'Do you ever think of anything else except football?'

'Are you mad?' chuckled Charlie. 'What else is there to think about?'

'Give it a few years son, and you'll be chasing girls around instead of a ball.'

'Uuugh!' heaved Charlie. 'Don't make me puke, da. Girls? Never! Nothing is ever gonna get in the way of my dream. I'm gonna go all the way! You wait and see. You'll be sitting in Old Trafford watching me score against City, one day.'

Charlie's dad put his arm around his son and pulled him toward him for a hug. Charlie liked that. He loved it that even though he was now twelve, his dad still gave him hugs.

'And poor oul me, son. I'll have to sit all on me own in the stands.' Then he chuckled. 'Ah, sure maybe Mammy will come and sit with me, knowing her son will be playing. I think that's the only way we'll get her into Old Trafford.'

'Or Granddad?' smiled Charlie, looking up at his dad.

Charlie's dad raised his eyebrows. 'Yeah, it'd be great if your granddad could see you out there. You know how much of a United fan he is. He'd be dead chuffed, son.'

Charlie sat down on a park bench. 'Sit down and tell me about Granddad.'

'What's to tell, son?' asked his dad.

'Come on, Da!' pleaded Charlie. 'Did he get you supporting United?'

Charlie's dad sat down.

'He did, son.'

'Go on,' said Charlie.

Charlie's dad laughed. 'I don't know what you want me to tell you son. You'd be better asking your granddad. He'd love that.'

Charlie felt like he was banging his head against a brick wall, trying to get his dad talking about Granddad. He'd thought that if he got his dad talking, then it would remind his dad of how important Granddad was to him and he might think of putting their differences aside, before Granddad went home the next day.

'Ah, Da, you're hopeless!' Charlie complained. 'You know, you two have me worried about yiz, don't you?'

Charlie's dad shook his head. He was a bit embarrassed.

'Ah, don't be silly, son. There's nothing to worry about there. Me and Granddad are solid.'

'You're not solid!' argued Charlie. 'Ever since that fight yiz had in Dublin, things haven't been good between yiz.'

'How old are you, thirty?' laughed Charlie's dad.

Charlie playfully pushed his dad's arm. 'Give over, I'm serious!'

'Look, son, sometimes grown-ups disagree about things and they find it difficult to well, agree to disagree.'

Charlie was furious. 'Where are you going with your "grown-ups" speech? I'm not four, you know.'

Charlie's dad was about to laugh again, but he knew by the look on Charlie's face, that this was really bothering him.

'I'm sorry, son. You're right. Look, I'll try and have a chat with Granddad before he goes home tomorrow, and see if we can clear the air.'

'Deadly!' Charlie punched the air.

'Don't get your hopes up, kid. Your granddad is a stubborn old mule. I'm not guaranteeing anything, okay?'

Charlie put his hand up for a high five. 'Give me some there!' smiled Charlie.

As Charlie's dad's hand slapped against Charlie's, *I did it!* Charlie thought. *That's FULL TIME on that problem.*

CHAPTER 6

TRAGEDY STRIKES

Later that evening, Charlie and his dad and Uncle Tony were watching *Match of the Day 2* to see if they could spot themselves on TV.

Granddad came in and sat down beside them. He had been upstairs helping Granny to pack for their trip home to Dublin.

'All right, Granddad?' smiled Charlie. 'I called up to tell you that it had started, about ten minutes ago.'

'I heard you, son,' said Granddad. 'You know your granny. Once a job is started, it has to be finished.'

Charlie's mum popped her head around the door, 'Anyone fancy a cuppa?'

Everyone raised their hands.

'Hey, Tony,' said Charlie. 'Come on and we'll help me ma with the tea.'

'You wha'?' gasped Tony. Uncle Tony was a little lazy; he had recently moved back in with Granny and Granddad because he'd sold his apartment and was heading off to Australia to take up a third-level teaching post. Since moving back in with his parents, he was used to Granny doing everything for him.

Charlie nodded to Tony and then he nodded toward his dad and granddad. They weren't paying attention. They were glued to the match.

'Oh, oh yeah! Yeah, that's a great idea. Sure your mammy can't be expected to do everything.'

Phew! Charlie thought. *Now Da can have that chat with Granddad.*

As Charlie was closing the door behind him, he coughed in his dad's direction to get his attention. It didn't work. Charlie coughed louder.

'You want a sup of syrup for that cough, son,' said Granddad without even taking his eyes away from the match. 'Honey and glycerine.'

'Right, thanks, Granddad. I'll do that,' said Charlie, and then he coughed again.

This time his dad did notice.

Charlie pointed toward Granddad and then made a chatter sign to his dad, with his hands, as if to say, *Now is a good time to have your chat with granddad.*

Luckily for Charlie, his dad knew what he was up to. He nodded and gave Charlie a thumbs-up. Charlie closed the door behind him.

Charlie and Tony stayed in the kitchen for a while. There wasn't a sound from the living room, bar the match. Charlie told his mum what he was up to so she didn't go in with the tea.

'Are you in on this plan?' Charlie's mum smiled to Uncle Tony.

'Who me? No!' chuckled Tony.

After about ten minutes Charlie eventually heard talking from the living room.

'Shush!' said Charlie. 'They're talking.'

'Come away from the door, Charlie,' insisted his mum. 'Don't be nosy.'

'*Don't be nosy*!' echoed Charlie. 'Are you mad? I'm dying to hear how it's going.'

Everything seemed to be going well until Charlie heard a change in the tone of conversation. Everyone heard the tone change.

'They're at it again,' said Tony.

'We don't know that,' said Charlie's mum. She felt sorry for Charlie, who now had his right ear pressed against the kitchen door.

Suddenly the voices stopped talking and Charlie felt the door pushing in. He jumped to his feet and in barged his dad, all stressed out and worked up.

'Flaming oul fool!' complained Charlie's dad. 'Any chance of a cuppa tea, love?'

Charlie's mum raised her eyebrows and turned to make a fresh pot of tea.

Charlie was gutted. 'What happened?'

'I told you not to get your hopes up, son, didn't I?' Charlie's dad was fuming.

It was a disaster. Charlie's plan had backfired and now there was an even greater wedge between his granddad and his dad.

* * *

Charlie said his goodbyes to his granny and granddad and Uncle Tony at breakfast. He had to go to school and they had an early flight home to Dublin. Charlie's dad had already left for work.

'Keep your chin up, kiddo,' smiled granddad as he gave Charlie a big hug.

Charlie didn't want to let go of Granddad. He felt terrible that things were now worse between his dad and his granddad, and somehow, he felt that *he* had made it worse by interfering.

As Granddad pulled away from their hug, he pressed Charlie's nose and clicked his fingers, just like he used to do when Charlie lived back in Dublin.

'I've got your nose now,' chuckled Granddad.

'Leave it out Granddad,' Charlie blushed. 'I'm not a little kid anymore.'

'Eh!' Granddad smiled. 'Don't you be in any hurry to grow up, Charlie. Before you know it, you'll be an oul crock like your granddad.'

'I'll see yiz all soon,' smiled Charlie. 'And Granddad,' Charlie winked. 'You're not an oul crock. I think you're mint.'

That meant the world to Granddad.

'I'll see you to the gate, son,' smiled Granddad. Just like Charlie, Granddad didn't want to say goodbye. 'You won't forget your oul granddad now, sure you won't, Charlie?' he said as he gave Charlie one last hug.

'Get off!' laughed Charlie. 'How could I forget you, Granddad?'

'You're a great lad, Charlie. D'you know that?' smiled Granddad.

'I'm a Stubbs, Granddad.'

'You better be off, now' said Granddad. 'You stick with your football. It's the best game in the world, and it's a true gift to be able and fit and healthy, to be lucky enough to play it. I wish I could still play. It was the happiest time of my life, playing football.'

'I know, Granddad,' smiled Charlie. 'Dad told me you were good. Don't worry. Next time I'm back in Dublin, you and me will go to the Lawns and have a good kick about, all right?'

Those words smothered Granddad's sadness with warmth and happiness and hope – great hope.

Charlie slung his school bag over his shoulder and headed off to school. As he came to the end of his street, he turned around one last time to see Granddad waving from the front gate. Charlie stopped and raised his right hand and gave Granddad a big thumbs up. Granddad did the same but with both hands and then turned and walked back up the path and out of Charlie's view.

* * *

Charlie's head was a complete mess in school. He should have been getting into trouble with his teacher for talking in class about the match in Old Trafford, but instead his mind wandered in class, worrying about two of the most important people in his life, and the morning passed by like a slow-drifting mist of gloom.

Out in the school yard, Charlie was in no mood for games. He usually joined in a kick-about up on the grass, but instead he just sat on his own, watching his pals play.

Charlie sat there for a good fifteen minutes undisturbed until the school secretary came scuttling across the school yard in his direction.

It wasn't until she got right up to Charlie that he realised that she was looking for him.

She sat down beside him.

This is dead weird! Charlie thought. *The school secretary never does this. Gosh! I'm just having a bad day. Aren't I allowed sit on me own? Leave me alone, why don't you.*

Then without any delay, she spoke.

'Hello, Charlie. You're needed in the office.'

'What?' asked Charlie. He was confused. 'For what?'

The school secretary blushed. 'Em! Your mum is there waiting for you, pet.'

'Me Ma? Nah! Not my ma, she's at the airport with my granny and granddad.'

There was no response from the secretary. 'Are you serious?' asked Charlie, just to make sure.

The secretary nodded.

Charlie jumped to his feet and followed the secretary across the yard and into the school main hall.

As Charlie approached the main office he noticed the school principal standing outside. He was nodding his head and he had a very serious look on his face, and then he went in to the office.

Oh crap! Charlie thought. *I must be in trouble. What have I done? I'm in for it.*

The office door was closed. The school secretary lightly knocked on it before opening it.

Charlie walked in behind her and noticed his mum sitting on a chair. She had tears in her eyes, but still she smiled at Charlie. The school principal was sitting in a chair opposite her. He had a sorrowful look. The office door closed.

'What's up?' Charlie asked.

The principal stood up. 'We'll leave you for a moment or two,' he gestured.

This is bad! Charlie thought. *This is very bad!*

The door closed and Charlie and his mum were left alone in the office. This had never ever happened before. One time, Charlie had fallen and hurt himself in the yard. His mum was called to the school, but they weren't left on their own in the office.

'Mum, what's happened?' Charlie asked. 'Is Da all right?'

Charlie's mum nodded. 'Of course, pet. Your daddy's fine. Come sit down.'

Charlie sat on the other chair. It was still warm from the principal sitting on it, but Charlie barely noticed. He had a cold shiver running up and down his spine, with worry. Charlie's mum reached out her hand and took Charlie's hand.

'It's your granddad,' she wept.

Charlie squeezed his mum's fingers. 'What? What about Granddad? Sure he's gone back home. He'll be up in the air now, maybe landed.'

Charlie struggled to hold the tears back. He knew that no matter how hard he tried to resist, the truth was the truth and his mum was going to tell him the truth.

I hope he's not dead? Charlie thought. *Please let him not be dead!*

'He's, he, well he wasn't feeling well after you left for school. He ...'

'Is he dead?' Charlie blurted, panic on his face.

Charlie's mum's eyes filled up and the tears ran down her face.

'No!' cried Charlie. 'He can't be. He was all right when we said goodbye.'

'I'm sorry, Charlie,' his mum wept. 'It was sudden. He just collapsed.' She wiped her face dry and pulled Charlie in toward her. Charlie knelt in front of her and rested his head on her shoulder, clinging to her coat. 'He felt no pain son – not an ounce.'

Charlie lifted his head and leaned back on his heels. 'What happened, Ma?'

Charlie's mum shook her head. 'We don't know, son. We won't know for a few days.'

'Where is he now?' gasped Charlie. 'Can I see him?'

Charlie's mum shook her head.

'He's gone to hospital in an ambulance. When they say we can see him, we'll bring you in.'

Suddenly, Charlie realised that he wasn't the only person who would be sad. 'Is Granny all right? And Da? Does Da know?'

Charlie's mum nodded. 'He's at the hospital with your granny now, son. Uncle Tony is there too.'

'Can we go?'

Charlie's mum shook her head. 'No, we'll go home love and wait for them there.'

'Okay,' said Charlie. 'I'll get my school bag.'

* * *

Charlie lashed his ball against the side wall of the corner house of his street. He was fed up sitting in with his mum, waiting for the others to get home.

With each strike of the ball he released hurtful rage and fury, shooting the ball against the crumbly bricks of the old end terrace house.

Why did this have to happen? Charlie thought, over and over again.

With one last strike, Charlie swiped at his football, sending it high, crashing through the upper landing window of the house.

Charlie grabbed his hair and began to pull at it as tears streamed down his cheeks.

An old man came ranting out of the house with the ball in his hands.

'Did you do that? I'll have you for that.'

Suddenly, Charlie's dad's car came down the road. He spotted the trouble on the corner of the street. He pulled in and asked his brother to drive their mother to the house. Charlie's dad apologised to the old man and explained the situation to him. Charlie was leaning against the side of the house – his head pointing toward the mossy ground. Charlie's dad put his arm around his son and instantly Charlie swung around and hugged him, sobbing into his dad's chest.

'I'm sorry, kid,' said Charlie's dad. 'I know you loved your granddad. We all did.'

Charlie lifted his head, 'You didn't get to make up, Da!'

Charlie's dad bit hard on his bottom lip, trying his best to hold back the tears.

'Listen here, son.' Charlie's dad brushed his hands through his son's hair to comfort him. 'Me and your granddad are solid. We always were and we always will be. Your granddad will be up there now, giving out about the two of us standing here sobbing about him. He wouldn't want that, son.'

'I'm sorry, Da,' said Charlie.

'Eh?'

'I'm sorry yiz didn't make up before he died. It's my fault for trying to force yiz to make up.'

Charlie's dad dropped to a hunch.

'No! Don't you ever think that like that, son. Do you hear me?'

Charlie nodded.

His dad pulled him in and hugged him tightly.

'I'll never fight with you, Da!' Charlie wept.

His dad patted him on the back.

'It's okay, Charlie. It's okay. Just like Granddad and me, we'll always love each other no matter what son, no matter what. Don't ever forget that.'

CHAPTER 7

BIG DECISION

The following week was tough for everybody. Because Granddad had died outside the country he lived in, he had to be what is known as 'repatriated'. Lots of forms had to be filled out to allow Granddad to be flown back home to Dublin, where he would be buried. Although there was lots to do and organise, this gave Charlie's mum and dad time to think about what had happened and what was best for the future.

They had come to a big decision.

While Uncle Tony and Granny were out walking, Charlie's mum and dad sat him down in the kitchen and had an important, life-changing chat with him.

'It's been a tough week, hasn't it kiddo?' Charlie nodded. 'Em! Look, there's no way of tip-toeing around this Charlie, but your mum and I have been talking about things and with Granny too and well, we've kind of made a big decision.'

'About what?' Charlie quizzed.

Charlie's dad looked to mum for help. He wasn't sure what way their news would settle with Charlie.

Charlie's mum was just as uneasy as his dad.

'You know Granddad worked in his shop all on his own?'

'Granny worked there too,' Charlie interrupted.

Mum smiled.

'That's true. Granny helped him from time to time, but not so much lately because of her arthritis. Well,' his mum continued. 'Em ...'

'Granddad always wanted me to take over his shop, Charlie,' Dad said

'You don't like the shop' said Charlie. 'That's why we left Dublin.'

Charlie's dad sat back in his chair. 'No, it's not. I liked working in the shop. Sure, didn't I work there when I left school?'

'But I heard you saying to Ma one day, that you were glad we left and that finally you had a chance to do something you wanted to do rather than something you had to do. And, I heard you and Granddad arguing about it too, when we were back in Dublin at Christmas.'

Dad looked at mum. She didn't know how to help with this.

'I didn't mean it like that, son,' his dad tried to explain. 'You see, I spent so many years working with Granddad in his shop, and I had never really got a chance to do something different, and well, when the chance came up to take the job here in Manchester, well, it just seemed the right thing to do. And well, yes, you're right, Granddad asked me again at Christmas if I'd move back and take over the shop. And yes we argued about it.' Charlie's dad put his hands to his face. He was upset.

'Sorry, Da,' said Charlie.

'It's all right son. I'm okay. I just need you to understand. Life's complicated. Not everything falls into place easy. Sometimes we have to just go with our hearts and that's not always the right path and yes sometimes it means being a bit selfish, but we have to do what we think is best and now that things have changed with, you know, Granddad, well, your mum and I have made this decision.'

'What decision?' asked Charlie.

Charlie's dad looked to his mum again.

'We're moving back to Dublin!' smiled Charlie's mum, but it was a nervous smile. 'Dad is going to run Granddad's shop.'

There was silence.

Finally, Charlie spoke up.

'But what about the trial with United, and my team and well ...'

Charlie's dad reached his hand across the table and grabbed Charlie's.

'Don't be worrying about your football, son,' he smiled. 'We can get you on a team back in Dublin and well, no matter where you're playing, that scout will still want you to go for your trial and sure lads from Dublin head over here for trials all the time. This won't affect your dream, Charlie.'

'Promise?' Charlie looked worried.

'I promise, son. Honestly, we can make this work.'

'You've plenty of friends back in Dublin, Charlie. They'll be delighted that you're moving back,' smiled his mum. 'What do you think, son?'

Charlie wasn't sure, but he loved his mum and dad and he didn't want to let them down. He trusted them, and if his dad said that everything would be ok and Charlie wouldn't miss out on his chance with United, then he believed him.

'Okay!' smiled Charlie. 'Let's do it.'

* * *

Charlie sat up in his bed that night. He couldn't sleep. He kept worrying about his trial and how he would miss his football team and all the kids he had made friends with over the past six years since moving to Salford from Dublin.

Charlie knew he was Irish. When he first moved to England he had really missed Ireland and all the friends he had left behind, but a lot of good came into his life since moving to Manchester. His football really took off and it was in Manchester that Charlie felt his football ability really developed. Now that he was moving back to Dublin, he worried if that would affect the way he played, and would he be able to settle into a new team and make friends all over again.

I suppose at least I still have the friends I left behind. Charlie thought. *I always hang out with Zucko and Ant when I'm home in Dublin for visits. But what team will I join? I hope I get me game? I hope that scout doesn't give up on me?*

Charlie *was* frightened but there was one train of thoughts which gave him comfort that night.

Dad's doing the right thing, Granddad. He's going back to look after your shop. That's what you wanted, isn't it? Miss you Granddad – love you always.

CHAPTER 8

FAREWELL TO A LEGEND

It took two weeks to sort everything out and finally bring Granddad home to Dublin to be laid to rest. Charlie said his goodbyes to all his friends and team mates from Salford Devils. His coaches were gutted to see him leave and they assured him that they would make sure to put the United scout in touch with Charlie so he could go for his trial.

Granddad's funeral was very sad. There were lots of people there, some young and some old. Granddad was very popular.

After the funeral, there was a gathering for tea and sandwiches back in Granddad's old football club, Ballyorchard.

'Come on with me, son, and I'll introduce you to a few of Granddad's old pals,' said Charlie's dad.

Charlie shook his head. 'Nah, you're all right, Da. I'll stay here with Ma.'

'Come on, kid. They're gas oul fellas. They used to play football with Granddad. You can tell them about your trial. They'll be all ears.'

Charlie perked up, 'All right then.'

There was great banter coming from the far table in the corner of the hall, next to the bar. Four men were sitting there and to listen to them, you wouldn't think they were at a funeral. This annoyed Charlie.

What are them oul farts laughing at? This is supposed to be a sad day Charlie thought as he followed his dad to their table.

The four men stood up and reached out their hands to Charlie's dad.

'Sorry for your loss, Tom,' said one of them, and as he bounced back onto his seat he let an enormous ripper of wind from his bottom.

'Oh, be Jaysis, I'm sorry.'

Charlie thought this was hilarious and burst out laughing.

All the men laughed, including Charlie's dad. This broke the ice.

'Ah, sure better out than in,' joked one of the other men.

'That's what old Tommy would have said, for sure,' smiled another. And he raised his pint of Guinness in the air. 'This one's for you, Tommy, rest in peace, old friend.'

Four glasses raised. 'Rest in peace, Tommy,' all four men paid their respects to their fallen pal.

Charlie's dad looked at Charlie and smiled. He was glad that he had brought Charlie over to this table to meet Granddad's old pals and to see how much Granddad meant to them.

'Sit down, Tom. Can I get yiz a drink?' one of the men asked.

Charlie's dad pulled over two chairs and he and Charlie sat down.

'No, God, you're all right, Paddy. Sure if I took a drink off every table, I'd be carried out of here.'

They all laughed.

'Is this your young lad, Tom?' Paddy asked, tipping Charlie on the arm.

'That's Charlie!' smiled his dad.

'Be Jaysis, he's the spit of Tommy,' said one of the men.

'And he's gone big – a right young man, indeed,' nodded another.

'He is that,' agreed Charlie's dad. 'He has his Granddad's touch on the pitch too.'

'Aw sure, we've been getting the full story on this fella from Tommy, ever since yiz went to Manchester,' smiled Paddy.

'D'you hear that, son?' Charlie's dad nudged him.

Charlie just smiled. He wasn't sure what to make of the conversation or where it was going, but if it had anything to do with football then it was worth listening to.

'He's got a trial for Man United coming up soon,' announced Charlie's dad – pride beaming from his face.

'Are you serious?' gasped Paddy. 'D'you hear that, lads? A trial with United.'

The other three men congratulated Charlie with a handshake.

Charlie was a bit embarrassed but deep inside, he was chuffed to bits.

'I'd say Tommy is up there now, Charlie and he's as proud as punch with that, son,' said Paddy. 'Did you know that your Grand-dad was a stunning footballer – offered a trial back in the day, himself?'

Charlie and his dad's ears cocked.

'A trial?' echoed Charlie's dad.

Paddy nodded, and then he took a gulp of Guinness. 'For sure.'

The other three men, nodded in agreement with Paddy.

Charlie looked to his dad. 'You never told me that Granddad had a trial in England.'

Charlie's dad raised his hands up with surprise written all over his face. 'He never told me. I didn't know that myself, son.'

'Ah, he had,' said Paddy. 'Didn't he, lads?'

'Tell us about it,' said Charlie. He was leaning over the table now – his two elbows dug in. This was interesting stuff – this was exciting stuff.

'Well, I know it wasn't Man United,' said Paddy. 'But it was a decent club, none the less.'

'Who was it?' asked Charlie.

Paddy turned to the other three men. 'Who was it again, lads? Can yiz remember? I can't remember for the love of God.'

'Blackpool!' announced one the men.

'Was it Blackpool?' asked Paddy.

'That's right,' agreed another. 'I remember there were two clubs looking at him – Blackpool and, ah, I think, Leicester was the other, but it was definitely Blackpool that offered him a trial.'

'D'you hear that, Da?' smiled Charlie. 'Granddad had a trial with Blackpool.'

Charlie's dad looked shocked and thrilled and very proud.

'Shame he didn't go,' said Paddy. The other men nodded.

'Shame – very unfortunate.'

'He didn't go?' echoed Charlie. 'Why?'

'His dad, your granddad, Tom,' Paddy looked to Charlie's dad. 'He took really sick at the time and sure Tommy was the eldest. He couldn't – wouldn't go swanning off to England for a football trial, so he didn't go. He took over his dad's shop and the rest is history.'

Charlie turned to his dad – disappointment on his face.

'Poor Granddad,' said Charlie.

'But at least he continued his football with the club and to this day he remained a loyal member. Blackpool's loss – our gain. He was a legend,' said Paddy. He raised his glass. 'To Tommy – a legend!' said Paddy.

'A LEGEND!' said Granddad's pals.

CHAPTER 9

FOUL PLAY

Charlie's mum had called into his old school and explained their situation to the principal who agreed to allow Charlie to finish out the last few weeks of school with them, before the summer holidays.

Charlie wasn't happy with this decision.

'This is stupid, Ma,' he complained as he put his coat on. 'There's only a few weeks left. Why can't I wait until September to go?'

'I'm not having you moping around the house and getting under Granny's feet. She's very upset over Granddad and Tony going to Australia yesterday has her worse, plus she has a lot of getting used to us moving in with her, and sure it'll do you good to catch up with your old pals. It'll be easier in September for you then.'

There was a knock on the door.

Granny opened the front door. There were two young lads, Charlie's age, standing there with school bags.

'How are you, Mrs Stubbs?' said one of the lads, with his head lowered.

'Hello, boys,' smiled Granny. She knew their heads were lowered because they didn't want to have to tell her that they were sorry about Mr Stubbs.

'Charlie!' Granny called. 'There's someone at the door for you.'

Who'd be calling for me? Charlie thought. 'I'm gone, Ma. See you later, Granny!' Charlie said as he closed the living room door.

Charlie was greeted with two big smiles. 'All right, Charlie – story? We thought we'd call in for you. Your ma told us that you were starting back in school.'

'All right, Zucko? All right, Ant?'

Zucko and Ant were two friends from around the corner. Charlie never forgot them when he moved to Manchester and they never forgot him. They always hooked up to play ball whenever Charlie was home. It took half the journey to school before either of the two plucked up the courage to mention Charlie's granddad.

'Sorry about your granddad,' said Ant.

Charlie nodded.

'Yeah, bud. He was sound,' said Zucko. 'You all right?'

'Yeah,' said Charlie. 'It was a bit of a shock, but I'm sort of getting used to him not being around now. Like, I didn't see much of him over the past few years anyway so I just pretend that it's just like the way it was. I haven't really thought about not seeing him again.'

'He be flying high, way up in de' sky. He be watching down, so don't you frown!' smiled Zucko.

Charlie laughed. Zucko always made Charlie laugh, 'Are you still doing them mad rhymes, you spacer?'

'He does me head in!' said Ant. 'He thinks he's Dr Seuss.'

'Dr Zucko!' laughed Charlie.

'I'm a literary poet – don't yiz know it?' laughed Zucko.

'Yeah, but you sound like a Muppet, so why don't you shut-up-it!' joked Ant.

The three pals were in stitches, walking through the gates of Charlie's old school.

This was good for Charlie – just what he needed.

They were early so they hung around the sheds until the bell went. Charlie had his ball with him so they had a kick about.

There was another game of ball going on, near the far side of the sheds, and when Zucko fired the ball against one of the shed pillars, it ricocheted and almost hit one of the other boys.

'Nice one!' complained Ant. 'You nearly hit Murph. You can get it!'

'I *will* get it' said Zucko. 'I'm not afraid of him. He's a thick.'

'I'll go with ya,' said Charlie. Charlie didn't like the looks that Murph was giving them so there was no way he was going to let his pal face him on his own.

'Are you coming?' Charlie asked Ant.

'Yeah! Course I am.' Ant growled.

Jake Murphy, AKA Murph, was not the most popular kid in school. In fact, Murph was not the most popular kid in Ballydermot. He had moved to Ballydermot just a year ago and he was nothing but trouble and everyone knew it. He only had a few friends and they were only hanging around with him because they were afraid of him. He was a brilliant footballer, but a dirty one – a hacker. He was trouble – big trouble and that's why he had recently left Zucko and Ant's team, Ballyorchard under 12's, just before the league finished.

Murph had Charlie's ball at his feet. He was rolling it back and forth under his left foot, and then he flicked it up between his two feet and began to do keepy-uppies.

'Can I have me ball back?' Charlie asked.

Murph ignored Charlie and just sniggered.

'Come on, Murph,' said Zucko.

'Give him his ball!' added Ant.

Murph trapped the ball under his left foot again and turned to Charlie.

'I don't know *you*. Who are you anyway?'

'Just give me the ball, will you, or do I have to come for it? I will if I have to,' Charlie warned.

Ant looked at Zucko, a very worried look.

'Don't get thick with me!' Murph snapped. 'Where are you from anyway? Not around here! You sound different.'

'He's *from* Ballyer,' said Zucko. Not like you.'

'Ballyer!' laughed Murph. His two pals joined in. 'He's not from Ballyer – state of him and his accent!'

'HE IS! IT'S YOU THAT'S NOT FROM BALLYER!'

shouted Ant.

Charlie was running out of patience. He was just about to step up to Murph's space when Murph did something that he normally wouldn't do. He rolled the ball over to Charlie.

Ant and Zucko were baffled.

Murph's backed down! Ant thought.

The Muppet! thought Zucko.

But that wasn't the case at all. Murph was clever, and he had just spotted the principal heading in their direction.

'Here's Gargamel!' announced one of Murph's pals.

Charlie swivelled around on his ball. 'Is he still alive?'

Zucko and Ant laughed, but they made sure that the principal didn't see their faces.

Murph turned his back on Charlie and proceeded to walk away as if there was nothing going on between them.

'Jake!' Gargamel called.

Murph kept walking, pretending not to see him.

'MURPHY!!' Gargamel shouted.

Murph turned around. 'What?'

'Into the office!' growled Gargamel.

As Murph walked by Charlie, he brushed off Charlie's shoulder. That was a warning. This wasn't over.

* * *

It didn't take long for everyone to know why Murph was called into the principal's office and when Charlie found out, he was livid.

'I'll burst him!' raged Charlie, on the way home from school.

'You're better off staying away from Murph,' Ant advised. 'He's a head banger. Just leave it, Charlie.'

Ant was level-headed like that and very mature for his age. Zucko on the other hand was not.

'I'd burst him' said Zucko. 'I wouldn't let him away with that – robbing Match Attax from your granddad's shop. I mean your da's shop, sorry,' said Zucko.

'It's all right,' said Charlie. 'It's sort of me da's shop now, kind of.'

'How much did he rob?' asked Ant.

'Two boxes!' said Zucko.

Charlie laughed. 'It wasn't two boxes.'

'How d'you know?' asked Zucko.

'I texted me da at break. It was only a few packets, but he's not happy.'

'What's gonna' happen to Murph?' asked Ant.

'Don't know,' said Charlie.

Just then, who should walk around the corner and straight into them, only Murph and his sidekicks.

'Ah, look who it is, the rat pack,' sniggered Murph.

'Who you calling a rat?' Zucko snapped. 'I'll deck ya.'

'Go on, you thick!' said Murph's pal.

Zucko dropped his bag to the ground.

Ant stood between the two of them. Ant knew that even though Zucko had the heart of a lion, he would be no match in a fist up with Murph's friend.

'Come on lads, leave it out!' said Ant.

Murph's friend backed off.

'We didn't rat on ya,' Ant said to Murph.

'You must have!' said Murph. 'He did anyway 'cos it was his oul fella's shop.' Murph pointed at Charlie.

'I'm not a rat,' said Charlie. 'And I'm not a thief either. You better give them Match Attax back.'

'Come on, Charlie, leave it,' said Ant. He was worried for his friend. Ant knew that they weren't in the school yard under the watchful eye of Gargamel, and he knew how mental Murph was.

'D'you think so?' grinned Murph. 'I'm gonna take your ball as well.'

Charlie had to think sharp. Murph was bigger than him, and Charlie knew, just like Ant, that Murph probably could overpower him.

He's not getting me ball, Charlie thought.

He dropped his ball to his right foot and before Murph could put in a block, Charlie swerved the ball across the road to where Zucko had run.

Zucko took the ball down on his chest and burst out laughing. 'Come on and get it, if you can – doubt it though.'

Ant joined in. As he went to run into a space to form a triangle, so the ball could be passed around easily, away from Murph, Murph lashed his foot out and caught Ant just above the shin.

'Aaaaaargh!' yelled Ant.

'You big eejit!' Charlie protested.

Murph and his pals laughed.

'That was a dive,' sneered Murph. 'Ant thinks he's Ronaldo.'

Charlie and Zucko helped Ant to his feet, but he could barely put his foot to the ground. Murph had done a proper job on him. Murph thought it was funny, but he wasn't laughing for long as his mam was out looking for him. Gargamel had managed to get in contact with her and told her all about his thieving from the shop.

Mrs Murphy came jogging down the road toward them. She was a runner – very fit – and there was no escape for Murph.

She dragged Murph off up the road and his pals quickly dispersed. They were puppies without Murph to front them.

Charlie and Zucko helped Ant back to his house. By the time they got there, Ant was walking better, but there was no way he would be able to take part in training that night.

'You should come, Charlie,' said Zucko.

Ant laughed. 'Are you mad, Zucko? Charlie's too good for our team. His da'll want him to join a premier side next season. Charlie's on trial with United, you dope. He's not gonna' join us, we'll be in 13 B.'

'Aw, yeah.' Zucko realised that Ant was probably right.

'I can play for who I want to play for!' said Charlie.

'You're gonna need to be playing in premier if you want to be heading off on trials for United,' explained Ant.

'I don't think so!' Charlie disagreed. 'Sure all leagues have good players. Don't be so quick to put your team down, pal. I'll have a chat with me da, all right?'

'Nice one!' smiled Zucko. 'I'll send a text to Terry. He's our manager. I'll let him know that you're coming up tonight.'

'Will he mind?' Charlie asked.

'Will he mind?' Ant laughed. 'His head will spin around and fall off when he hears that you're coming up. Everyone knows about you, Charlie. He'll be delighted.'

CHAPTER 10

BACK IN ACTION

As Charlie walked through the gates of the Lawns' playing fields, he got a flashback to the morning when Granddad brought him there to watch his dad play a football match for the Ballyorchard senior team. Now Charlie was about to train with the same club. His dad didn't mind, when he asked him if he could go training with them.

'I don't mind who you play for, son,' smiled his dad. 'As long as you're happy. It'd be nice to keep the family tradition going. Sure the season is over now. Train with them and we'll sort things out later in the summer, before the leagues start up again.'

Charlie had knocked around for Zucko and Ant early. He couldn't wait to get back in action.

Ant's leg was still sore, but he thought he'd tag along anyway.

'We're early,' said Zucko, as the three pals climbed the Lawns' sloped grassy mound, near the main road.

'Look! There's no one here yet. Come on and we'll roll down the hill.'

'Terry's there,' said Ant.

'Don't mind Terry,' said Zucko. 'He's setting up the grids.'

Zucko threw his water bottle on the grass, and he dropped flat on his back.

'Bombs awaaaaaaaaaaay!!!' cheered Zucko as he rolled down the hill.

Charlie laughed and then looked at Ant. 'Zucko's mental!'

As Zucko staggered to his feet – his legs wobbling and his head spinning – a girl in football gear and boots ran in through the gates and whistled in Zucko's direction.

Zucko spun around and fell back on his rear end. The girl burst out laughing.

'Zucko, you mad banana. You wanna sort your head out or you'll never keep up with me in training.'

Zucko blushed, and jumped straight to his feet. 'Go on out of that. I'd run rings around ya!'

'Yeah, right!' the girl smiled and as she ran up the hill and past Ant and Charlie, she smiled in their direction. 'All right?'

Ant nodded with a smile. Charlie just stood there, his jaw hanging and his eyes bulging.

'Who's *that*?' whispered Charlie. He was intrigued by the girl's confidence and vibrant personality.

'That's Kelly,' said Ant. 'Kelly Murphy.'

'She's all right, isn't she?' chuckled Charlie. 'Does she play for your team?'

'Yeah! She could have played for the under 14's girls' team, but she wanted to stay in her own age group and I think she likes playing on our team.'

Zucko had managed to drag himself back up the hill and shake all the loose grass from his hair. He didn't get it all out as some of it was stuck to his hair gel. 'D'you fancy her?' he laughed.

Charlie spun around. 'No, I don't. Will you give it up, you sap.'

'Go on, Charlie, you do fancy her,' Zucko persisted.

'Shut up, Zucko' Charlie smiled – his face reddening. 'The state of you anyway. There's all grass on your head.'

'Yeah,' laughed Ant. 'You look like me granny when she gets up in the morning – her hair looks like that – all fuzzy.'

'SICK!' heaved Zucko. 'Don't compare me to your granny – the smell of her.'

Ant laughed. 'Yeah, she does smell a bit.'

'All grannies smell!' laughed Zucko.

'Will yiz shut up!' laughed Charlie. 'Yiz are doing me head in.'

Zucko patted Charlie on the back. 'Come on and we introduce you to your new girlfriend.'

'Cop on!' snapped Charlie. The joke was going too far now. He'd be mortified if Zucko started joking like that around Kelly. It was hard enough to go training for the first time with a new team without having the pressure of his pals winding him up and playing tricks.

'I'm only messing,' said Zucko. 'Sure, you wouldn't want to be hanging around with her, anyway.'

'Why?' asked Charlie.

Zucko looked at Ant. 'Did you not tell him who she is?'

Ant shook his head. 'What difference does that make?'

'Who is she?' quizzed Charlie. They were starting to freak him out.

'Kelly Murphy,' said Ant.

'I know, you muppet,' smiled Charlie. 'You told me that already.'

'*Murphy!*' echoed Zucko.

Charlie was baffled. He raised his hands up. 'Sooooooo?'

'Murphy, as in Murph!' said Ant.

'Oh!' said Charlie. 'She's Murph's sister?'

'*Twin* sister!' said Zucko.

'Twin?' Charlie gasped. 'No way!'

'I know!' chuckled Zucko. 'It's a real case of beauty and the beast, isn't it?'

'Come on,' said Ant. 'There's loads up now and Terry's after telling Don to get everyone warmed up.'

As the three boys jogged over to join the rest of the team, Charlie glanced over toward Kelly. Kelly smiled at him, but Charlie dropped his head and pretended not to see her.

He didn't like doing that. That's not the way he was brought up, but Murph was trouble – big trouble, and Charlie had already figured out that no matter how much he thought he had liked Kelly at first, he didn't need nor want to be around trouble.

Zucko introduced Charlie to Terry. The manager extended his

hand and shook Charlie's.

'How you kiddo? You all right?'

Charlie nodded with a smile. He was nervous, and Terry could sense that.

'Delighted to have you with us, Charlie' said Terry. 'Listen, there's no pressure on here. The season's over and we're just keeping the training going, so you just do your thing.'

'Thanks,' said Charlie.

Don had set the team up in a circular grid, just passing the ball around, to warm up.

'This is Charlie,' Terry said to Don.

'Ah, I know your daddy and I knew your granddad,' smiled Don. Don was soft and all the players liked him for that.

As Ant was injured, he was still standing beside Charlie. Zucko had joined the rest of the team.

'He's on trial for United!' Ant announced.

Charlie nudged Ant's arm.

'We know all about that,' smiled Terry.

'Good man, Charlie,' smiled Don. 'A superstar training with us – how lucky are we, Terry?'

'Listen, Don, will you take Charlie over to the rest of the team?' asked Terry.

Don nodded.

'I just want to talk to Ant about his injury.'

'They're a sound bunch of players,' Don told Charlie. 'I know it's not easy being the new kid, but you'll be grand, all right? Okay, ball in!' Don called. 'Listen up everyone. This is Charlie – he's a new player, so I want yiz all to welcome him aboard, all right?'

Everyone nodded and some even extended the nod to a slight wave. Kelly did neither. She didn't like it that Charlie had blanked her, when she had smiled at him earlier.

'Are you on trial with United?' asked Nailer.

Charlie just nodded.

'Class! Shame it's not with Liverpool though,' Nailer joked.

This started a bit of banter between some of the players. There was a mixture of United, Liverpool and Chelsea supporters on the team.

'I told ya!' Charlie heard to his left. 'He must be good?'

'All right, all right!' Don interrupted the whispers. 'Look! Charlie's one of the team now, so he's here to help us out and we're here to help him out all right, come on now, on your toes.'

Everyone jogged on their toes, and even though they were focused on Don, the whispers still continued to pass around the team. Never before, had they trained with a player, who was on trial with a Premiership club in England, or any club in England. Their expectations would be very high, and Charlie knew this. He was now under more pressure than he had ever been under before.

* * *

Charlie gulped a mouthful of water. The grids were good and they were hard. Charlie loved that. He loved to train hard. He was competitive and even though he knew that the leagues for his age group were classed as non-competitive, Charlie always pushed himself to the limit. That's the way he was made – that's the drive he had in him, and that would never change for Charlie – football was life – football was the air he breathed to live each day.

Don had set up two goals for a match. There were now fourteen players on the team, with Charlie, but as Ant wasn't training, and two other players, Lee, the goalkeeper, and Johnner weren't there, there were eleven for the match.

'We'll have six and five,' Don informed Terry.

'No probs, bud,' said Terry. Terry was handing out the bibs to the players.

'Here, put Charlie on the team with five,' said Griff.

'Yeah, he's easily two players,' chuckled Tobo as he walked off with a red bib.

Don handed a red bib to Charlie. 'You all right, kid?'

Charlie smiled. 'Sound.'

'Good man,' said Don. 'Don't mind the chit-chat. That'll wear off soon enough.'

Charlie was picked to be on Zucko's team. Don did that deliberately so Charlie would have someone familiar, playing beside him.

'You know them all, don't you, Charlie?' Zucko asked. 'That's Seany, Tobo, and that's Nailer.' Zucko pointed his team out to Charlie.

Charlie nodded.

He was on the team with the five players. The reds were strong, but so were the blues. They had Heno, Davo, Griff, Filly *AKA* Boots, Ali and Kelly.

'Okay, yiz have twenty minutes of a match so let's get it going!' said Terry.

'Is it all in?' asked Seany.

Terry looked to Don. Don nodded as if to say, *sure why not?*

'All in!' announced Terry as he dropped the ball to Tobo's feet.

'Reds are fly goal keeper,' said Don.

Tobo knocked the ball back to Zucko, who took a touch and passed it back to the last man, Seany. Seany was a very calm and collected defender. There was no thumping long passes up front. Seany changed direction and passed it across to Charlie who had taken up position out on the left wing.

Charlie had a decision to make. It was all in. That meant that if he wanted he could take on as many players as he wanted. But did he want that? He felt that he could beat them all. He had watched them train in the grids and he had already figured out for himself that he was a class ahead of most of them. There were a few strong and talented players on the team, particularly Nailer who was well known for his skill on the ball and clinical hard tackling. But did that give Charlie the right to show off? Of course it wouldn't be showing off deliberately, but that's probably the way it would be seen.

I'll play it cool! Charlie thought and just as he turned inside, to pass the ball to Nailer, Charlie felt a crunching tackle into the back of his legs.

BANG!

Charlie hit the ground.

Don thought Terry's head was going to explode, he was blowing so hard on his whistle.

Charlie had just been clobbered by Kelly.

As Charlie stood up, he noticed Terry calling Kelly to one side. Terry wasn't pleased with the tackle.

'You all right, kid?' asked Don.

Charlie nodded. 'Sound – it didn't hurt. It wasn't that bad.'

Charlie could hear what Terry was saying to Kelly – something about her brother and the way he used to carry on in training and his bad tackles too.

'That's not like you, Kelly,' Charlie heard. 'Go on over to Charlie and shake his hand,' said Terry.

Kelly walked over to Charlie as he stood over the ball.

'That was a hack job!' Zucko protested.

'Leave it,' said Don.

'Sorry,' said Kelly. She stretched out her hand.

'Sound,' nodded Charlie.

Kelly stepped back a few paces to allow Charlie to take the free kick.

Now I believe she's Murph's twin, Charlie thought as he checked through the corner of his eye, if Kelly had calmed down or if she was still wound up.

Charlie quickly put the bad tackle behind him and he got on with doing what he did best in life – playing football.

He scored four goals and assisted another three.

The red bibs beat the blue bibs by a score of 7-4, even with only five players. Tobo was almost right earlier, when he said that Charlie was the equivalent of two players. In fact, Charlie was amazing. He controlled the ball in the centre of the pitch and he was involved in all the play going forward and defensively.

Terry and Don couldn't believe what they had seen. They had the highest regard and respect for each and every one of their players, but they knew that it's not very often, if ever, that a coach gets to see a young player with Charlie's talent.

Don called all the players in, when training was over. Terry was busy talking on his phone.

'Listen up now. We're gonna have a match on Saturday.'

'Deadly. It's about time we had a friendly. The league's over ages.' Filly interrupted.

'Good man, Filly,' smiled Don. 'I was chatting to a pal of mine, the Rosco Boys' manager and he's decided that he's gonna keep the training going with just a short break of a couple of weeks for the summer so we thought we'd have a friendly between both teams – no harm there,' said Don.

'I have to go to a wedding,' said Griff.

'No worries, Griff,' smiled Don.

'But they're two leagues ahead of us,' said Tobo, completely ignoring Griff's disappointing news.

'So?' said Seany. 'We'll still hammer them.'

'Did yiz ever see their centre mid, Hallo? He's some player.'

'Aw, he's deadly,' added Griff. 'Class player.'

'Here, Kelly,' laughed Heno. 'You'll get to play against your brother.'

Kelly's brother Murph had joined Rosco Boys at the end of the season since he had left Ballyorchard.

Kelly never flinched.

'All right, enough of the banter,' said Don. 'Look, it'll be a good match just to finish off the season and then there's gonna be a disco in the club hall later that night, all right?'

'Go on, Ant,' laughed Heno. 'You better get your leg better for the disco.'

'Yeah, Ant the disco king!' laughed Griff.

All the kids joined in. Ant had a reputation for disco nights. His moves on the dance floor were even better than on the football pitch.

'Go on out of that!' smiled Ant.

'Okay! Very good!' laughed Don. 'Look, it's on from seven to ten as usual, but messing aside, be up for a quarter past eleven on Saturday morning for the friendly, kick off is twelve. Now go on, see yiz then – safe home.'

As Charlie walked out the gates of the Lawns with Zucko and Ant, Terry asked Don, what he thought of the new player.

'He's a class act, that kid,' said Don. 'You can see his old man in him. He was a decent player too. I played alongside him for a good few years.'

'I bet he wasn't as good as Charlie' smiled Terry as he squeezed the last ball into the bag.

'He was brilliant,' said Don. 'But that kid is special. You don't see that often in one lifetime. I can tell you that.'

'I can't see him signing for us,' said Terry. 'He'll go premier next season, for sure. You wait and see. Once word gets around about him, they'll be all after him.'

'You'd imagine,' agreed Don, and he zipped up the training bag and stood up and smiled to Terry.

'You never know Terry. His family has deep roots in this club. His poor oul grandda, Lord rest him in peace, was a Legend for the club, back in the sixties. He might just want to play for us. He seemed to settle in well tonight.'

Terry laughed. 'Yeah! Except for Kelly's warm welcome into the back of the legs.' Don laughed too. 'Watch that space,' said Don. 'Watch that space.'

CHAPTER 11

HIDDEN TROPHIES

Charlie decided to call in to Granddad's shop on the way home from training. It was a Thursday night and Charlie's dad had the shop open late.

Zucko and Ant still had to do their homework so they headed off home.

There was nobody in the shop, and Charlie's dad was out in the back room, rustling through some of Granddad's old notes and stuff, belonging to the shop.

'Are you there, Da?' Charlie called out as he raided the box of fizzy cola bottles.

'I'm in the back, son.'

Charlie found his dad in behind a cupboard, pulling out bits and bobs that were covered thick in dust.

'Mother of God!' gasped his dad. 'Your granddad certainly was a hoarder. There's stuff here from the eighties.'

'What are you doing?'

'I'm just having a root around, son. The shop is quiet all night and I thought I'd clean up back here.'

Charlie laughed. 'You mean you're having a nose?'

Charlie's dad smiled. 'Something like that.'

Charlie was still buzzing from training and he wanted to let his dad know how it went.

'So you settled in all right then?'

'Yeah! It was sound, Da.'

'Was Don training ya?'

Charlie nodded. 'He's bang on, Da. Dead nice! Terry's all right as well though. Knows his stuff, if you know what I mean.'

'I know him,' said Charlie's dad. 'They're two good lads, Charlie. You'll do all right, son, playing ball for them two.'

'So can I join the team then?' asked Charlie.

Charlie's dad was on his knees. He looked up. 'I told you already son, you can play football for whatever team you want.'

'Sound, Da,' smiled Charlie. 'I can't wait to tell Zucko and Ant.'

'Hello?' a voice called out from the shop.

Charlie's dad jumped up and dusted himself off.

'Back in a minute, son.'

Charlie looked around in the store room while his dad served the customer. There was a lot of old stuff there. Charlie's dad was right when he said that Granddad was a hoarder.

Charlie noticed that in behind an old vending machine, there was an open archway. It was very dark and Charlie couldn't see a thing. He rummaged around behind the vending machine for a light switch, and eventually found a cord hanging down. He pulled the cord and the archway lit up.

Charlie peeked in around the machine. His eyes bulged with curiosity.

'Where are, ya?' Charlie's dad was back.

'I'm around here!' called Charlie. Charlie's dad snuck his head around the wall.

'What are you up to?'

'I'm trying to move this yolk!' strained Charlie. 'Give us a hand?'

'What are you up to? Are you mad?'

'Come on, Da!' gasped Charlie. 'There's a secret room behind this.'

Charlie's dad laughed. 'That's not a secret room. That's just where Granddad used to keep bits of shelves and rubbish like that.'

Charlie's dad grabbed a hold of the vending machine and on the count of three, father and son pushed the big obstacle to one side and opened up the way to Granddad's 'secret room'.

Charlie dived straight in. His dad was right. There were lots of old pieces of shelving and boxes of nuts and bolts and a lot of other boring stuff, but Charlie spotted an old leathery sports bag sitting on the bottom shelf, tucked away in the corner.

Charlie grabbed the bag.

'Man, this is heavy.' Charlie dragged the bag across the floor of the little room and stopped it at his dad's feet.

Charlie's dad knelt down beside him.

'I never saw that before.'

There was something sticking out of a side pocket. Charlie pulled it out. It was an old photo – a very old photo of two football teams.

'That's your granddad,' pointed Charlie's dad. 'Wow! That's his old team. Now that's an old photo.'

'Are they all dead?' Charlie asked.

His dad laughed. 'I don't know, son. I wouldn't say so. Sure didn't you meet a few of them at the funeral?'

'Oh, yeah,' Charlie chuckled.

Charlie grabbed hold of the bag's zip. 'Let's open it. It might be treasure.'

Charlie's dad laughed and he nudged his son, playfully. 'Treasure? Granddad wasn't a pirate.'

As Charlie slowly zipped the bag open, his heart raced and he wondered what wonderful treasure might be inside.

'Wow!' Charlie gasped.

'I don't believe it!' said his dad as he reached into the bag. 'Granddad's football trophies.'

'Granddad's hidden trophies!' smiled Charlie. 'And an old football. I've never seen one like this before. It must be ancient.'

Charlie's dad took the ball and squeezed it with both hands. 'We'll have to try and pump it back up. I'm not sure if it will work though. It's very old. But look at the signature on it.' Charlie's dad handed the ball back to Charlie.

'I don't believe it!' gasped Charlie. 'Is that Bobby Charlton's autograph?'

'Certainly looks like it, son!'

'How did Granddad get that?'

Charlie's dad shook his head. 'I didn't even know he had this ball, Charlie, never mind it being signed by United's greatest legend. You hang onto that ball. Granddad would have wanted you to have it.'

'Thanks!' smiled Charlie. 'I'll keep it forever – promise.'

This was exciting stuff. Charlie had just heard stories about how good a player Granddad was and his trials in England and now *he* had found Granddad's football trophies – his hidden football trophies, and the mysterious old football signed by Bobby Charlton.

'Did you not know any of these were here?' Charlie quizzed.

Dad was baffled.

'No – no I didn't. I mean, these must have been here even when I worked in this shop all those years ago. He never said. I mean, I remember him showing one or two to me when I was young like you, but not a whole bag of them.'

Charlie pulled out trophy after trophy and medals too.

'If I had all of these, I'd have them up on a shelf or over the fireplace where everyone could see them.'

Charlie's dad smiled and then he chuckled. 'That wasn't your granddad at all. He was very humble and very shy at times. It wouldn't have suited him to show them off.'

'But that's what they're for.'

'No, not for everyone, son. These were Granddad's trophies, and Granddad knew how special they were and, I suppose, that was enough for him.'

Charlie and his dad emptied the whole bag and lined Granddad's old trophies along the dusty floor. There was one small one still stuck in the bottom of the bag. The footballer's head was caught in the inside pocket. Charlie carefully pulled it out, and he read the inscription at the bottom.

LEGENDS' LAIR Champions 1966

'What's that mean, Da?' Charlie handed the trophy to his dad.

Charlie's dad gazed at the inscription for a moment. Charlie thought he could see a tear form in the corner of his dad's eye.

'You all right?' Charlie put his arm around his dad.

'Smashing,' his dad smiled – his voice trembled.

'Do you know what it means?' Charlie asked a second time. 'What's the Legends' Lair?'

Charlie's dad stood up and went to the front of the shop. He closed up for the night and when he returned to the secret room at the back of Granddad's shop, he sat down with his son and he told him all about the Legends' Lair.

'It was unbelievable. I wish you'd seen it. The atmosphere was second to none. Football, son – it was all about the football. I mean the pitch itself was nothing to boast about. It was just a tarmacadam seven-a-side pitch in the middle of a square of houses – nothing fancy. But it was the football. There were great tournaments there every summer. Teams used to come from everywhere.'

'Why was it called the Legends' Lair?'

Charlie's dad smiled. 'They said it was where legends were made and legends played.'

'I don't get it?'

'Young and old,' his dad added. 'You could have oul former players like your Granddad, well maybe not that old, and you could have young players play in it too. It was a cracking tournament on a cracking pitch. None like it, anywhere else.'

Charlie held up his granddad's trophy. 'Granddad must have won the tournament with his team that year.'

'He must have, son.'

'I wish I could play there. Is it still around? Does the tournament still run?'

Charlie's dad shook his head. 'I'm afraid not, son. The days of tarmacadam and concrete pitches are well gone. It's all astro turf now.'

'Why not?' Charlie was devastated. He wanted to follow in Granddad's footsteps.

'It's a rundown, disused area now. It was sold years ago to a developer and before he got a chance to build on it, the recession hit and that was that. It's just a rundown piece of land now. All the houses around it were sold too.'

'I want to see it, Da,' said Charlie.

'I'm not sure about you going there, Charlie. D'you hear me, son? It's all boarded up. I don't think it's even safe to go in there. Best keep away from it, okay?'

Charlie nodded, but his heart was set on seeing the legendary football pitch where Granddad had won his most precious trophy of all.

I've got to see the Legends' Lair! thought Charlie. *But first I need to find out where it is? Maybe Zucko and Ant will know? I'll ask them tomorrow.*

CHAPTER 12

THE LAIR

Charlie brought Granddad's ball to school with him, the next day. Even though dad had managed to inflate it again, Charlie knew that this was no ordinary football and he would have to take good care of it. He was dead proud of his granddad and all his football achievements, and he wanted to tell everyone about the hidden trophies he'd found.

Charlie pulled out the old photo of Granddad and his team, from his back pocket, at lunch time.

'Giz a look,' said Zucko. 'What century was that taken in?' Zucko laughed.

'Give it back,' smiled Charlie. 'It's not that old.'

'Not that old,' gasped Ant. 'Look how young your granddad is in it.' Ant looked at the photo again. 'Which one is your granddad anyway?'

They all laughed.

'Ant, you muppet,' said Charlie. 'That's him there.'

'Were they really that good?' asked Zucko.

Charlie nodded. 'Legends.'

'Go on!' chuckled Ant.

'They were!' insisted Charlie. 'You should have seen the bag of trophies I found last night in me granddad's store room at the back of his shop.'

'How many?' asked Zucko.

'Loads!' said Charlie. 'League ones and cup ones and there was one that was different to the rest. It was for a tournament on a pitch called the Lair.'

Suddenly, Zucko's head lifted from the photo. 'I know that place. Me oul fella always talked about it.'

'Yeah, mine too' said Ant. 'It was meant to be a savage place for football, like famous like.'

'Legendary?' said Charlie.

'Yeah, that's it,' said Zucko. 'The Legends' Lair – I heard that.'

'I wanna go and see it' said Charlie.

Ant looked at Zucko and Zucko looked at Charlie.

'What?' asked Charlie.

'It's in bits, you mad banana!' laughed Zucko.

'I know – me da told me that last night' said Charlie. 'I don't care. I still wanna go.'

'Fair enough,' shrugged Ant.

'So, yiz know where it is?'

'Of course we know where it is? *Everybody* knows where the

Lair is.'

* * *

Charlie, Zucko and Ant all sent text messages to their mums, telling them that they were going to drop into the park on the way home for a kick-about. Charlie made sure that Zucko had his ball with him – they wouldn't be playing with granddad's old ball.

Charlie hated the fact that he was telling lies, but he felt if he wanted to get to see the Lair then it was the only way.

Just like Charlie's dad had described, the Lair was in the centre of a square of boarded up houses. The three pals had to jump over an old security fence and thrash their way through a laneway riddled and overgrown with tall weeds and stingers and nettles, and as they emerged out the other end, Charlie had mixed emotions with what he saw.

'What d'you think?' asked Zucko. 'I told you it was in bits.'

Charlie leaned against the wall of one of the houses.

'I don't know,' said Charlie.

'What d'you mean you don't know?' asked Zucko.

'I'm trying to visualise it as it would have looked in its glory days,' said Charlie.

'It's a kip!' said Ant.

'No,' said Charlie and he moved away from the wall and walked toward the mossy and weedy Lair, with its rusted goal posts at both ends and glass-strewn tarmac with patches of worn paint which once lined the legendary pitch. 'This could be great again,' gasped Charlie as he turned to face his pals.

'You what?' laughed Zucko.

'Are you blind or something'?' laughed Ant. 'It's a dump. Who'd want to play football here?'

'I would!' smiled Charlie. He put his granddad's football on the ground and took Zucko's ball and set his eyes upon the near goal.

SMACK!

Charlie curved a sweet shot toward the old goal posts, smacking it against the cross bar.

'Nice shot!' said Ant.

'I'm surprised it's still standing!' chuckled Zucko.

'Exactly!' said Charlie.

'You're not making sense, Charlie,' said Ant. 'Will you give it up? It's Zucko's job to not make sense, not yours.'

'You muppet!' said Zucko, pushing Ant over, playfully.

The two pals began to wrestle. Ant had just got Zucko into a head lock, when Zucko noticed that Charlie had gone off up the Lair and and left them.

'Ah! Let me go!' cried Zucko. 'Come on, Charlie's gone, you thick, let me go.'

Charlie was standing at what used to be, the half way line. Charlie had played a lot of seven aside games for his dad's job's team back in Manchester, just for fun, and he had a good idea of what size a seven a side pitch would be, but the Lair seemed a little bigger.

'What did you mean when you said "exactly"?' Ant asked Charlie.

Charlie smiled.'Zucko thought that the goal posts should have fallen over when I hit the cross bar.'

Ant looked to Zucko. Zucko looked to Charlie. This was a regular occurrence between the three of them.

'So?' Zucko raised his arms.

'So, exactly,' smiled Charlie.'It didn't.'

Zucko returned his eyes to Ant. Ant shrugged his shoulders.

Charlie laughed. 'You two are spanners, d'yiz know that?' There's nothing wrong with this pitch. It's still the Lair. It's still the legendary football pitch that held loads of deadly matches and tournaments.'

'It's in bits' said Ant.'The state of it.'

Zucko looked at Ant and smiled.

'What are you smiling at?' asked Ant.

'So is your hair when you get up in the mornings!' said Zucko.

'What are you on about?' asked Ant.'You're a nut job.'

'No, I'm not!' chuckled Zucko.'I get Charlie, now. It's like your hair in the morning. It does be in bits, but then you fix it and it starts to look better, a bit of gel and that and hey presto! Just because this pitch is a wreck doesn't mean it's not a pitch. It's still a football pitch. It just needs fixing – like your hair in the mornings.'

Ant wasn't impressed with Zucko comparing his hair to the Lair.

'You're a dope, d'you know that?'

'Nice one, Zucko,' laughed Charlie. 'Weird but true.'

The three pals hung their bags on the old railings to the side of the pitch and they had a kick about with Zucko's ball. Charlie had figured in his head that at least if they did have a game of football, they wouldn't be completely telling lies, except they were in a different place, and not the park.

Ant was in goal. His leg was still badly bruised from Murph's bad tackle. Charlie was crossing passes to Zucko who was practising his headers.

'On the volley, this time Zucko,' Charlie called from the corner of the pitch.

'Move out then,' said Ant. 'You're too close, Zucko.'

Zucko moved back a few yards and waited to pounce on Charlie's cross.

SWISH!

Charlie sent a perfect ball into Zucko. Zucko leaned back and ....

Ant burst out laughing. Zucko had completely missed the ball.

'Here, Zucko, have another go!' called Ant as he picked up granddad's old ball. He threw the ball out to Zucko.

'Nooooooo!' yelled Charlie. But it was too late.

THUMP!

Zucko mis-kicked the ball and sent it high and wide toward one of the old rundown houses.

'Me granddad's ball!' cried Charlie.

'Crap!' Zucko covered his face with his hands.

The ball had gone over into one of the gardens of a house. The three pals ran over to have a look.

'It's like a jungle in there,' said Charlie. 'We'll never find it. I'm dead.'

The house was surrounded by straggly overgrown hedges. The gate was boarded up and there was a lock on its handle.

Charlie pulled on the gate, but it was no use. 'How are we gonna' get in?'

Zucko peered in through a small hole in the boarding. 'I don't think it matters whether we get in or not.'

'Why?' asked Charlie.

'Take a look for yourself,' said Zucko.

Charlie took a look. 'Ah, come on? No way.'

'What is it?' asked Ant.

'It's a dog,' said Charlie.

'A dog?' laughed Ant. 'So what?'

'Have a look,' said Charlie.

'OOH! That's a big dog!' said Ant.

'What's it doing in there?' asked Charlie. 'I thought nobody lived in these houses anymore.'

'They don't,' said Ant.

'Eh! That's not quite true,' said Zucko.

'What?' asked Charlie.

Zucko told Charlie and Ant how his dad had told him that there was still one person living in the old houses surrounding the Lair.

'An old man,' explained Zucko. 'He's a spacer.'

'But why is he still living here?' asked Charlie.

''Cos he's a spacer,' laughed Zucko.

'But it's all boarded up!' said Ant.

'Yeah,' agreed Charlie. 'Like how's that then?'

Zucko shrugged. 'I don't know everything. Maybe he doesn't want anyone getting in. like, or maybe he never comes out. I don't know. I'm just saying, he must live in there. That's why there's a dog in the garden – that's all.'

Charlie took another look in through the hole. 'What am I gonna do, lads?'

Zucko patted Charlie on the shoulder.

'Don't worry, pal. We'll sort it.'

'How?' asked Ant. 'There's no way in. There's a big dog that probably is as mad as its owner. How are we gonna get the ball back?'

'The dog looks well looked after, all right, so the old man probably takes him into the house at night. There's no sign of a kennel in the garden.'

'So how do we get the ball?' Ant asked.

'We'll come back tomorrow night before the disco is over, and we'll get it then,' said Zucko. He had it all worked out.

'What about tonight?' asked Charlie. 'I don't want to leave granddad's ball out all night. It's very old. What if it rains?'

'I can't tonight,' said Zucko. 'We're going to my grannies.'

Charlie looked to Ant.

Ant shrugged his shoulders. 'Can't, bud, we're going to the

cinema.'

'Leave it until tomorrow night' said Zucko. 'The ball will be sound for tonight and sure tomorrow night is perfect for us to come back.'

'Yeah, but we still have to get in there and the gate is locked,' worried Charlie.

Zucko smiled and he looked upward.

'What?' asked Charlie and Ant together.

'We'll go over the hedge,' said Zucko.

Ant looked to Charlie and Charlie looked upward. Zucko's plan wasn't perfect, but it was the only plan they had. It was agreed. Before the disco was over, they would come back to the Lair and go over the hedge.

I have to get Granddad's ball back Charlie thought. *Dad can't find out.*

CHAPTER 13

SURPRISE!

Charlie banged the last of the muck from his football boots and threw them into his bag. His mum and granny were out the front waiting on him. They were going to look after the shop while his dad went to watch Charlie play for his new team.

'Are you right, Charlie?' his mum called.

'I'm coming, Ma,' Charlie appeared at the front door.

Granny had a big smile on her face.

'What's so funny?' Charlie closed the front door and threw his training bag over his shoulder.

'Come on and you'll see,' chuckled Granny.

Charlie hadn't seen his grandmother in such good form since Granddad's passing.

He could see his dad peeking out the window of the shop. As soon as he spotted his family coming, he disappeared in a flash.

'What's Da up to? What's going on? It's a surprise, isn't it?'

Mum smiled at Charlie and nodded.

'Beast!' said Charlie.

'That's a new word!' chuckled Granny.

'Is it new football boots?' asked Charlie as they approached the door.

Mum shook her head. 'You only got new boots a few months ago.'

Charlie pushed the door open with his back. He was still hounding his mum and gran to let him in on the surprise.

'About time!' said his dad.

Charlie spun around, 'What's me surprise, Da?'

Charlie noticed that the three old men that he met at Granddad's funeral were in the shop and they were smiling and one of them was nodding toward the far wall to the side of the magazine stands.

Charlie glanced over to see what he was nodding at. The wall was covered with a sheet. 'What's going on?'

Charlie's dad grabbed a hold of the sheet. 'Are we ready?'

'Go on, Tom' cheered Paddy, Granddad's old pal.

Charlie's dad pulled the sheet down, revealing three shelves lined with Granddad's old trophies. They were polished and gleaming, and sitting up on show for all to see. Above them hung a framed picture of Granddad and his old Ballyorchard team.

Charlie was gobsmacked and speechless.

'Well? What d'you think, son?'

Charlie slowly walked toward the magnificent display, reading every inscription on every trophy.

'Your granddad would be chuffed to bits, Charlie,' said Paddy.

Charlie turned around. 'It's deadly. I love it.'

'I knew you'd be happy, son,' said his dad. 'You didn't want them stuck in the back.'

'D'you think Granddad will mind?' worried Charlie.

Charlie's dad shook his head.

Charlie noticed that there was a small shelf beside the others, with nothing on it. 'What's that for?' he asked

'This is the best bit, Charlie' said dad and he nodded toward Paddy. 'Will I tell him Paddy or do you want to?'

Paddy stepped forward. He had cramp from leaning on the counter., 'Oh, Jaysis – me hip,' he moaned. 'No, I'll tell him, Tom.'

'We'll be here all day,' laughed one of Granddad's other pals.

'The boy has a match to get to,' joked another.

'Okay,' said Paddy. 'I won't harp on.'

Charlie sat up on a counter. He was all ears.

'The match,' Paddy began. 'The one that trophy in the middle was for.'

'Don't be talking in riddles,' chuckled one of the old men.

'Will yiz let me tell him,' snapped Paddy.

Charlie laughed. *Granddad's old pals are head bangers* he thought.

'Where was I?' Paddy had forgotten.

'The trophy in the middle, Paddy,' smiled Charlie's dad.

'Oh, yeah,' said Paddy. 'Anyway, yeah, that's right, the trophy in the middle. Eh! Oh yeah, that was for winning the Legends' tournament in the Lair back in, in ....'

''66!' said one of the men.

Paddy turned around. 'Are yiz gonna' let me tell him?'

'Please,' smiled one of the men. 'Before St Peter comes in to the shop.'

Now Charlie's gran and mum and dad were laughing.

Paddy continued. 'To cut a long story short, Charlie, your granddad, Tommy, our pal, was handed the match ball, from the final in the Lair, when we won the tournament that year, in 1966.'

'He scored a hat-trick!' added one of Granddad's pals.

'That's classic,' gasped Charlie.

'Paddy was telling me that it's the ball that was in the bag with the trophies,' said Charlie's dad.

'That's mint,' smiled Charlie. 'Do you know anything about the autograph from Bobby Charlton?'

'Ah,' smiled Paddy. 'Well son, Sir Bobby Charlton joined Waterford City back in the mid seventies.'

'Waterford City!' Charlie echoed, gobsmacked.

'I know!' chuckled Paddy. 'It's hard to believe, but he did. He only played a few games for them. Anyway, your granddad being a big United fan and a big Bobby Charlton fan, brought his ball to one of the matches and managed to get Charlton to sign it after the game.'

'It's worth a few bob now, that ball,' said one of Granddad's other pals.

'It's priceless,' said another. 'There'll never be another like it.'

'I thought it would be nice to place it on that shelf, Charlie, with the other memorabilia,' smiled Charlie's dad.

Suddenly, Charlie's face went grey.

'Are you, all right, pet?' asked Granny

Charlie slid down off the counter. 'Eh! Yeah, grand,' he smiled. It was a fake smile, disguising his horror. 'Eh! I haven't got it with me.'

'Of course you haven't,' said his dad. 'No worries, son. Sure we can come back with it later, after your match.'

Charlie's dad shook Granddad's pals' hands and thanked them for dropping into the shop to see the memorabilia.

Charlie waited outside for his dad. His mind was racing. *What am I gonna do?* he fretted. *I better get that ball back, and quick!*

As Charlie sat on the shop window ledge, shortly afterward, Paddy appeared beside him, his pipe in hand and his cap in the other.

'I didn't really get to tell yiz the full story,' smiled Paddy.

Charlie looked up. 'What?'

Paddy lit his pipe and began puffing.

'That ball,' spluttered Paddy.

Charlie sat patiently awaiting Paddy's next words.

'That ball,' Paddy continued. 'Oh, that ball, there was terrible ructions over that ball.'

Charlie's brows raised. 'What d'you mean, Paddy?'

'Well, now don't get me wrong, son. Your granddad, Tommy, deserved that ball. He sure did. He was without doubt, man of the match on the day, and of course he got his hat-trick.'

'And when you score a hat-trick, you get the match ball,' Charlie added.

'That's right, son,' smiled Paddy.

'Then why was there trouble?'

Paddy took a puff from his pipe. 'There were two hat-tricks scored in that final.'

'Two?' gasped Charlie.

'Two!' echoed Paddy. 'The score was 5-3, I think – something like that if I remember correctly. And I can tell you this, the other hat-trick scorer wasn't happy with the decision to give the match ball to your Granddad. He felt he should have walked away with it, that day.'

'Who was the other player?' Charlie was intrigued.

Paddy paused.

Just as Charlie was about to ask that question again, his dad came out of the shop.

'Ah, that doesn't matter,' shrugged Paddy. 'All water under the bridge now.'

'Come on, son, we better get going.'

'All the best!' Paddy tipped his cap.

Charlie was fascinated with Paddy's story. *I wonder who the other player was,* he thought as he watched Paddy slowly disappear into the butcher's shop, three doors down.

'Come on, Charlie. Are you coming?' Dad called.

Charlie ran alongside his dad.

'Listen, son,' said dad. 'You won't go anywhere near that Lair, sure you won't?'

'Why are you asking me that?'

'I'm just saying again, son, that's all. You know like with Paddy's story in the shop, about it all. I don't want it getting you all buzzed up again and wanting to go in there, okay?'

Charlie nodded.

This can't be happening! Charlie thought as he looked up at his dad. *I better get that ball back.*

CHAPTER 14

BALLYORCHARD V ROSCO BOYS

Terry and Don had the goals up and the pitch ready for the friendly, the last game Ballyorchard would play as an under 12's team. Under 12's matches allow nine players on each team to start as opposed to eleven-a-side, which you'd have in under 13's upwards. At Under 12's, the pitch isn't full size either. This is all to do with player development; a smaller pitch with fewer players allows more player participation, creativity and goal-mouth action with more chances to score. Next season Charlie and his friends would be under 13's and they would step up to a full-sized pitch.

Rosco Boys were warming up behind the top goal, opposite end to the dressing rooms. Terry called all his players down to the dressing rooms to get their jerseys on. Charlie took his boots from his bag and handed the bag to his dad.

'Mind that for me, Da,' said Charlie.

'I'll be over at the line son. Best of luck, kid – enjoy yourself out there, that's the important thing.'

Charlie nodded and ran down the slope after his team mates.

The dressing room was small and stank of old grass. All the players squeezed in beside each other along the narrow wooden seating.

There was great atmosphere. Everyone loved playing matches. That's why they trained so hard and put all the effort in, week in and week out. It was all for that short time, once a week on the pitch, and it was worth it.

'Okay, everyone, listen up!' said Don. 'We're just gonna go through the team here.'

'Where's Johnner?' asked Filly.

'He's still sick,' Terry lifted his head from the training bag. He was sorting the jerseys out. 'Griff's not here either and Ant's leg is still dodgy so we have eleven today.'

'I'm grand,' said Ant.

'Are you sure?' asked Terry. 'You didn't look like you were walking too good on it.'

'Yeah, it's sound,' insisted Ant. 'Sure I was kicking ball yesterday,' Ant looked to Charlie who was sitting beside Zucko, 'Wasn't I lads?'

Zucko nodded.

Yeah, the ball that we couldn't get back thought Charlie. *Thanks for reminding me, Ant.*

'Fair enough,' smiled Don.

'Right. The team,' said Terry. 'Will you hand out the jerseys, Don?'

Don grabbed the jerseys from the bag.

'We know who the keeper is,' Terry smiled, and he continued to call out the team. 'Ali, left back, Seany and Heno centre half and Davo, right back.'

Don handed them, their jerseys.

'Kelly, centre mid, Tobo right mid and Nailer, left mid, and Zucko is starting up front.'

'What about Charlie?' asked Ant.

Charlie blushed. He appreciated his friend's concern, but he didn't expect to be starting his first match with a new team.

Don handed out the last of the jerseys. 'Everyone will get a game,' said Don. 'You know how it works, not everyone can start every week. You have to take turns. You're all part of a team and everyone will get plenty of ball.'

'Okay, yiz know your positions,' said Terry. 'Ant, are you sure your leg is all right?'

Ant nodded.

'Okay, we'll bring you on after a few minutes.'

Terry looked to Charlie and Filly too. 'You'll all be going on after a few minutes, okay? Roll on, roll off.'

The three players nodded.

'Right,' smiled Don. 'We'll go up and get warmed up.'

There was ten minutes to kick off. Don and Terry laid out a fairly basic diamond-shaped grid with four cones for warm up.

There was a player on each side of the diamond and a line of players at either end. The front player on each line would pass their ball to the right sided player then receive a pass back from the side player. The player would then pass the ball to the next player waiting in the opposite line and then join the end of the queue. After a couple of minutes the players to the sides would swap with two players from the lines.

The purpose of this grid was purely warm up; nothing too strenuous or tiring.

When they finished, Terry called the team in to a circle to have a final pre-match chat.

'Did yiz see Hallo taking shots on their keeper?' Ali asked the others.

'Keeper didn't save any of them,' chuckled Davo. 'I feel sorry for you, Lee.'

'Go away outta that,' shrugged Lee. 'That keeper looks rubbish anyway.'

'He's a deadly keeper,' insisted Kelly. 'I watched him in a couple of matches. He saved two pennos.'

'So?' Lee wasn't impressed.

'Okay, enough,' smiled Terry. 'Look, let's concentrate on what we can do, and we know that we can play ball, don't we?'

'Yeah!' muttered some of the players and some gifted Terry with a mere nod and shrug of the shoulders.

'What's up, guys?' asked Don. 'Come on, where's the spirit? Are yiz up for this game or what?'

Don was trying his best to get his players going.

'Yeah, come on, lads,' Zucko stood up. 'Come on, we're gonna beat these.'

Zucko's enthusiasm was infectious.

'Yeah! Come on, lads!' added Seany.

Suddenly all the players were up on their feet.

'Come on then everyone,' said Terry. 'On your toes.'

The whole team started jogging on the spot.

Terry went through the positions again with all the players; just a few words of encouragement to each player. He reminded his defence of how important it was to mark tight and if they were to break forward, they must get back quick. Seany was allowed to go up for corners.

The midfield were encouraged to work hard and get the passing right and tight, and Zucko was reminded to come and seek out passes. Filly was told this too for when he would come on. Although Filly was a superb centre forward, he had a tendency to tuck in beside the opposition's centre half, waiting for the perfect pass to his feet, which kind of worked well for Filly as he was top scorer for the season.

Once the referee had checked the players' boots and had his little chat with them, it was time for the two captains to meet in the centre circle.

Terry and the Rosco Boys' manager thought it would be nice and unusual if they made Kelly and Murph their captains for the match.

The brother and sister, twins, smiled each other down in the centre of the pitch.

'Yiz haven't a hope,' smirked Murph.

'No need for that,' said the referee.

'It's all right, ref,' smiled Kelly. 'This loser is me brother.'

'Interesting,' smiled the referee. 'I don't want any fighting out there – keep it clean.'

'He can do what he wants,' chuckled Kelly. 'He won't get near me. I'm too quick for him. I'll just skill him.'

The referee smiled and looked to Murph for a reaction, but Murph just stood there, eye-balling his sister.

'Right then,' said the referee. This was definitely a first for him. 'We'll get it going.'

Charlie jogged over to where his dad was standing.

'I'm sub,' smiled Charlie.

'That's sound, son,' smiled his dad. 'First game, no bother, kid,.

'The two captains are twins,' said Charlie.

'You're kidding!' Charlie's dad thought that was amazing. 'Are you serious? And they play for different teams.'

'Murph, the fella, used to play for us but he left. Kelly's sound – deadly player,' said Charlie.

Charlie's dad patted his son on the back. 'Your oul granddad would be dead proud of you today, son, playing for his old club.'

Charlie nodded and smiled. He missed Granddad, and he thought of how lucky he was for Granddad to see him play in his last match in Manchester.

* * *

The first ten minutes of the game were very tight and you couldn't say which team was the stronger. They were equally matched, player for player. Ballyorchard's expectations of Hallo were spot on – he was class and he moved the ball around the centre of the pitch with pinpoint accuracy and when the Ballyorchard's mid-field tried to string passes together, it was Hallo, backed up by Murph, who broke down their play and sent their team on the attack.

The first corner of the game came to Rosco Boys, as Ballyor-chard's left back, Ali, slid in to block a cross from the Rosco's right mid.

Hallo ran over to take the corner. He had a wicked right foot on him for crossing the ball.

'Mark up!' Don called to his players.

'In tight!' called Terry. 'Tobo – Nailer, goalside, lads.'

Hallo took a glance and made some kind of gesture to Murph, who was lurking around the box. Kelly was marking him, but as Hallo crossed the ball in, and Murph made his run, Kelly slipped. Hallo's cross had venomous pace, and all Murph had to do was make good contact with it and it would be unstoppable.

BANG!

Murph headed the ball into the back of the Ballyorchard net.

GOAL!

The Rosco players ran over to Murph to celebrate.

Hallo jogged over, calm and collected. He was like that; he wasn't one to over-celebrate or do anything that might run down the opposition. A smile and high five from Hallo to Murph was enough in Hallo's book.

Murph was the opposite. He taunted Kelly as he jogged back to the centre circle.

Kelly was fuming – her brother scoring was a worst-case scenario for her, but she had to quickly put it behind her and get on with the match.

Before Ballyorchard kicked off, Terry signalled to the referee. With ten minutes to go in the first half, Terry and Don made two changes. They put Ant on for Ali at left back and Filly replaced Zucko, up front. Charlie would get his chance at half time.

Filly *AKA* Boots was wearing a brand spanking new pair of the brightest most reflective yellow boots anyone had ever seen before. Filly loved his boots. He would go through at least two or three pairs each season, but these new ones had to be the most provocative football boots that Filly had ever turned up with, as every time he made a run down the line, the sun reflected off his boots, blinding the Rosco defence.

'Go on, Filly!' came shouts from the Ballyorchard sideline.

'Go on, Filly – skin him!!'

Filly was on fire, his pace was breathtaking as he darted around the Rosco right back and sent a low bullet of a pass into the box.

Nailer trapped Filly's pass perfectly and super-skilled the Rosco centre half, back-flicking the ball into the path of Kelly.

SMASH!

Kelly struck the ball into the top left corner of the net.

GOAL!

It was one all.

The whole Ballyorchard sideline erupted. Charlie and his dad jumped up and down celebrating. Ant jumped up on Charlie's back.

'Go on Ballyorchard, woooohooooo!'

Now it was Kelly's turn to stare down her brother in the centre circle. Murph showed no emotion. He was completely expressionless.

Rosco had just tipped off when the referee blew his whistle.

It was half time.

Don called all the players in. 'Come on, get a drink everyone.'

'Come on, bring your drinks in!' added Terry.

Everyone huddled around Terry and Don.

'Super stuff out there!' Terry congratulated.

'You'd never think they were a couple of leagues ahead of us,' smiled Don.

'WE'RE GONNA BEAT THEM!' exclaimed Zucko.

'Good man, Zucko!' said Terry. 'That's the spirit.'

'Lads,' said Don. 'We have to keep the marking tight, all right? Everything else is sound. We can't fault yiz. Yiz are playing a stormer out there.'

Charlie stood just outside the group, listening in. Terry lifted his head and shifted his eyes in search for Charlie.

'Right,' said Terry. 'We'll keep the changes we made before half time for the moment and I'm putting Charlie on.'

Terry rolled his eyes from player to player, eventually stopping at Kelly.

'Kelly,' said Terry. 'Smashing goal – super work rate out there. I'm gonna give you a rest, okay?'

Kelly nodded and gulped back a mouthful of water.

Charlie glanced over to Kelly. He was hoping that he wouldn't be replacing *her*. He felt bad from training on Thursday and badly wanted to make amends for being so rude. No matter how hard Charlie tried, Kelly resisted making eye contact.

The referee gave a signal to both lines and everyone returned to their positions.

Don called Charlie over before he ran onto the pitch.

'Be yourself out there, kiddo,' smiled Don. 'Don't go holding back now.'

Charlie smiled. He appreciated that from Don as sometimes it wasn't easy having so much expectation on his shoulders and worrying about letting others down.

Don's kind words settled Charlie's nerves, as the new Ballyorchard midfielder took up his position in the centre of the pitch with Nailer.

'All right?' smiled Nailer.

'Sound!' smiled Charlie.

The referee dropped the ball to Charlie's feet. It was Ballyorchard's tip off.

'When you're ready, lads,' said the ref.

Charlie rolled the ball to Nailer and nodded. Nailer acknowledged Charlie. He had no problem letting his new team mate receive the first pass of the second half.

Just before the referee blew his whistle, Charlie shifted his eyes toward Hallo. Hallo nodded in recognition of Charlie's presence on the pitch. The Rosco star midfielder had heard all about the much-talked-about player, on trial with Manchester United.

As the referee signalled one more time for the tip off, Charlie made eye contact with Murph. Murph had a face on him like a bull ready to charge as soon as Charlie had the ball, but Charlie was one step ahead of Murph. As Nailer passed the ball, Charlie skilled both Murph and Hallo as the two Rosco midfielders moved in to take the ball from him.

Everyone in the Lawns who had come over to the pitch to watch the match and see exactly how good this so-called football prodigy was, were not disappointed as Charlie pulled off a Zinedine Zidane manoeuvre, leaving both Murph and Hallo mesmerised in the centre of the pitch.

'Did you see that, Zucko?' Ali gasped.

'That was beast!' smiled Kelly.

Charlie passed the ball out to Tobo. Tobo took one look at his opponent, took a step over and dropped his right shoulder. This was a manoeuvre that Tobo was famous for. The Ballyorchard number ten eased past his marker, and passed the ball back into Charlie. Charlie already had a great sense of what was going on around him. He knew that Murph and Hallo were on his heels and also knew that Filly had come inside to his left. Charlie did a step over and let the ball nutmeg through his legs and the Rosco centre half's legs.

'Nice one!' Filly acknowledged as he ran with the ball toward goal.

Filly was through.

SMACK!

The Rosco keeper dived to his right and just about got the tip of his fingers to Filly's shot.

'Great save!!' cheers came from the Rosco sideline. 'Up the Rosco!'

Charlie ran over to take the corner and Filly ran with him, but the Rosco right back was tight on Filly's heels.

'Send it in, Charlie,' said Terry.

Filly pulled away, taking the Rosco defender with him.

Everyone was marked tight in the box. Charlie looked to see if Seany was going to make a dash forward, but Terry had asked him to hold back as Heno was tying his boot laces and there were two Rosco players hovering around the half way line.

SWISH!

Charlie curled a cracker of a ball into the box. It missed everyone, including the Rosco keeper, and ended up in the back of the net.

GOAL!

What an amazing impression Charlie had made in his debut

match. Jaws hung and tongues wagged along the sidelines, all conversations about the wonder boy who had returned from across the seas with talent never seen in Ballydermot before.

The game settled down and so too did Charlie. Hallo got stuck in and upped his game, and he and Charlie had a remarkable contest of skill and pure football ingenuity in the centre of the pitch. Murph let Charlie know that he wasn't as impressed as everyone else, by niggling away at Charlie's ankles. He was on his last chance from the referee.

With five minutes to go, both managers made their final changes. Terry had already put Zucko back on for Filly and Ali back on for Davo, and now he was putting Kelly back on for Tobo.

Ballyorchard had a free kick just inside the Rosco half. Charlie nodded to Kelly to take the free.

'I'll go right mid if you want,' said Charlie, suggesting to Kelly that she take up her usual centre mid role again, now that the two of them were on the pitch.

Kelly smiled at Charlie. Charlie was delighted. He had finally got Kelly back on his side again.

Kelly took one look toward goal and surprisingly switched the ball across field to Charlie. Charlie took the ball down with his chest and controlled it beautifully with his left foot, clipping it over the Rosco left mid who had run toward him. Charlie was away down the line. He took a glance at goal and hit a cross into the box. The Rosco centre half beat Zucko to the ball and kicked a long clearance up the pitch.

Hallo was lurking just inside his own half. He had been tying his laces and didn't make it back to defend. Nobody had paid any attention to him. The Rosco number seven pulled off a classic back heeler, passing the ball to his forward. As Seany moved in to block him down, the Rosco number ten clipped the ball past Seany, back to Hallo. Hallo had just one defender to beat – Heno.

Heno was strong and he was a class defender. Not many players could get past Heno and there was no way he was going to let Hallo past him, but Hallo had more than just a few tricks up his sleeve and wanted to show Charlie and everyone else that Charlie wasn't the only player who could skill an opponent.

Hallo ran with the ball down the right hand side of the pitch. He knew Heno was right footed. Just as Heno was about to make his tackle, Hallo back clipped the ball in behind his left leg, nutmegging Heno on the inside. Halo surged past Heno toward goal.

Hallo took one last look at goal, and as Lee came off his line to block him down, Hallo chipped the Ballyorchard keeper.

GOAL!

Hallo had made it two all.

He's good! Charlie thought as he looked over to his dad. Charlie's dad was clapping his hands and he wasn't the only one on the Ballyorchard sideline who was clapping.

'Smashing goal!' said Don as he clapped in acknowledgement.

'Give it up, Don!' Davo protested. 'Whose side are you on?'

'Pure class, Davo!' said Terry. 'It's only a game, kid. That was class.'

The referee blew the final whistle and both teams lined up in the centre of the pitch. The match had finished two all. A great result for the Ballyorchard players against a quality team, who had thought before the game that they would easily beat their opponents from the lower league.

As Charlie put his hand out to shake Murph's hand, the Rosco midfielder pulled his hand away.

'You're a thick, d'you know that?' Kelly was in line behind Charlie.

Murph just laughed at Kelly as he walked by.

Charlie turned to Kelly. 'It's fine. It's his problem.'

'It will be,' said Kelly. 'When I tell me da.'

'It's all right' smiled Charlie. 'Don't do that. It's not worth the hassle.'

Terry and Don were ecstatic with their team's performance as they thanked them and their parents on the side of the pitch, for such hard work and commitment throughout the season.

'Yiz are a great bunch of supporters' said Terry. 'There's no bad words or trouble from yiz, I have to say. We appreciate that, honestly. We have to remember, it's all about supporting the kids and their football. Some teams have terrible trouble coming from the sidelines but we never get that from you guys and credit too to the Rosco supporters, who have been amazing. So, a big thanks for that from myself and Don and the club.'

Everyone appreciated Terry saying that. They understood what he meant as they had seen the bad behaviour of some supporters from other teams, screaming abuse and negative comments from sidelines at players and referees. That wasn't acceptable and clubs and coaches were doing the best they could to discourage and condemn it.

'Don't forget the disco tonight in the club, seven to ten,' said Don as everyone dispersed.

Suddenly, that little corner of the Lawns' playing fields was once again vacant and all that remained were the stud marks in the turf of yet again another great game of football.

CHAPTER 15

THE CLUB

Charlie was in his room, applying the last few bits of clay to his hair, when his dad knocked on his door.

'Are you in there, son?'

'Come on in!'

Charlie grabbed his hoody and pulled it over his head. It was his favourite, a Hollister one that his granny had bought for him for his birthday. Charlie only ever wore it on special occasions and tonight's disco was indeed a special occasion.

'All set?' smiled Charlie's dad.

'Yep! Just applying the last few finishing touches, Da.'

Charlie's dad sat on the edge of the bed. 'Ah, I remember the club discos when I was a kid. That's actually where I met your mammy.'

'Leave it out, Da!' laughed Charlie. 'I'm not going tonight to meet a girl.'

Charlie's dad laughed. 'I know, son, I was much older. Don't mind me, I'm only reminiscing. Anyway, I've to pop back down to the shop. I have it in my head that I left the light on in the back room, so if you have Granddad's ball handy, I'll pop it up on that shelf with his trophies, if you like?'

Charlie froze.

'What's up?' asked his dad.

'Nothing' said Charlie. 'Eh! It's eh, I don't—'

'You left it in school, didn't ya?' smiled his dad.

'What? I mean, yeah, that's right. I left it in school yesterday when I brought it in to show everyone. I'm sorry. I should have told you that, today in the shop.'

'No bother. Don't be worrying about telling me stuff like that, Charlie.'

Charlie's dad put his hand up for a high five.

'Sorry, Da, okay,' said Charlie.

'Go on then,' said his dad as he left the room. 'Off to the club with ya, and be back sharp now. No hanging around on the roads after it.'

Charlie plopped onto the bed. *I have to get Granddad's ball back.*

* * *

Charlie met up with Zucko, Ant and a few of his other team mates as he was heading down to the club.

All the pals were in great form and really looking forward to the disco.

'Here, lads,' laughed Ant. 'If there's any good looking girls here tonight, don't be surprised if yiz see them gathering around me, all right?'

Everyone burst out laughing.

'Ant, you spacer!' Zucko was cracking up and he started to rhyme. 'They be dancing and you'd be chancing, cos' the Ant is slick – no wait a minute, I meant to say thick.'

Zucko put his hand in the air toward his pals. 'Come on, give me some. Make it high.'

Even Ant couldn't resist giving Zucko a high five for that.

'Sure there'll be no girls here tonight,' announced Charlie. 'Well maybe Kelly, but she'll be the only girl.'

'No, you're misinformed, my good man,' smiled Ant. Ant saw himself as a bit of a girl-magnet. 'Terry told me that the club was open to all the teams tonight.'

'So?' asked Ali.

'So, that means the girls' under 14's might be there,' Ant had a smile on his face as wide as Dublin Bay.

'Aw, d'you think so?' gasped Filly. 'That means Rihanna Redding might be there.'

'She's a class footballer,' said Nailer.

'I heard she's a class snogger,' laughed Ant.

All the boys burst out laughing.

'Go on Ant, the Ballyer Casanova!' laughed Davo.

Charlie was in stitches. He hadn't laughed this much since he was back in Manchester.

The club was teeming with boys and girls. Ant was right. The under 14's girls' team were there and most of them had brought friends with them too. Ant's eyes were bulging as he scanned the entire hall.

'Ant, close your mouth, you're drooling!' joked Nailer.

'They're giving out drinks and crisps over there,' Charlie pointed. 'Anyone up for some?'

'Are you off your head?' said Ant. 'I'm onto the dance floor. There's women out there missing out on me moves.'

'You mad banana!' laughed Davo. 'I'm not going near that floor with you. You'll make a show of us all.'

'You should see him dancing,' said Zucko. 'He's beast.'

Nailer laughed.

'I am!' said Ant. 'Seriously!'

'Yeah, Ant, right!' laughed Filly. 'Go on then, show us.'

'I hope you're better at dancing than football' added Nailer.

'There's Kelly,' said Charlie as Kelly and her brother walked into the hall.

'What's Murph doing with her?' asked Ali.

'Look who else is here,' said Filly.

'What are they doing in our club?' asked Zucko.

Most of the Rosco team had turned up for the disco.

'Come on and we tell Terry,' said Zucko. 'He's over there. There's no way they're staying.'

'Leave it Zucko,' said Charlie. 'What's the problem?'

'This is *our* club!' protested Zucko.

'Chill out, Zucko,' said Davo.

'Ah, come on and we get drinks,' said Nailer. 'Don't mind them.'

'Yeah, come on, lads. The rest of the team is over there already. We better get stuck in before everything's gone,' said Filly.

Charlie tucked in behind his pals on the queue. He noticed that Kelly was walking over toward them.

'All right, lads?' smiled Kelly.

Everyone nodded.

'All right, Kelly?' smiled Charlie. 'You up for a dance?'

Kelly leaned her head right back. 'You what?'

'I'm only joking!' chuckled Charlie.

'I thought you were serious,' smiled Kelly.

'I'm not into dancing,' said Charlie. 'Not like Ant.' Charlie nodded toward the dance floor. Ant had made his way onto the floor and was putting his moves into action.

'The state of him!' laughed Kelly.

Zucko was in front of Charlie.

'Ant!' Zucko called out, but Ant didn't hear him. The music was too loud.

'ANT!!' Zucko roared at the top of his voice.

Ant gave Zucko a thumbs-up and broke into a dance that looked like a robotic moon walk, as he clattered off everyone who dared get in his way.

'Go on, Ant!' cheered Kelly. 'You're beast.'

Charlie thought that Kelly was impressed with Ant's dance moves and he wished that she would think the same way about him. 'I might get up after all,' Charlie turned to Kelly.

'Nice one,' smiled Kelly. 'Then I'll have two big eejits to laugh at!'

Charlie swiftly twisted his head back into line with the queue.

Maybe I'll leave Ant up there on his own! Charlie thought. *I don't want Kelly thinking I'm a big eejit.*

* * *

The night flew in and Charlie had a great time. It was nine thirty and Charlie had it in his mind that he should leave early to give himself plenty of time to try and get his ball back from the old man's house in the Lair.

Kelly had got fed up hanging around with all the lads from the team and she had gone over to the girl's under 14's team who were dancing at the far end of the hall.

Most of the lads had broken up and were scattered around the hall. Zucko and Filly were standing against the wall glaring over at Rihanna Redding. Charlie was with them for a short while but he felt uncomfortable as he noticed Rihanna and her friends pointing toward him and giggling.

Ant was making his way around the floor. He hadn't left it once since they arrived, not even to get a drink or go to the toilets.

Charlie tried to signal Ant to let him know that he wanted to head off. Ant was unreachable. There was no getting his attention. You'd think he had been transported into a *Just Dance* game and the only way you could make any contact with him was if you had a controller in your hand.

'I'm heading off, Zucko,' Charlie whispered into Zucko's ear. He didn't want Filly or anyone else knowing why.

'Why?' Zucko asked.

Charlie leaned in again. 'Me granddad's ball. I'm gonna' go and get it back. Me da keeps asking about it.'

'All right,' Zucko nodded. 'Get Ant and we'll make a move.'

Charlie knew that if he was going to get Ant's attention then he would have to go onto the dance floor and physically remove him from it, but he was worried that Kelly might think he was up dancing and he remembered how she joked about that earlier.

'You get him, will ya?' Charlie pleaded with Zucko.

'I'm bursting for a slash,' said Zucko. 'Get him and we'll go then.' Zucko disappeared through the crowd.

'Will you move out of the way, Charlie' said Filly.

'What?' asked Charlie.

'You're in me way,' snapped Filly. 'I can't see Rihanna properly.'

Charlie stepped aside and a big smile beamed across Filly's face.

'You're sad Filly, d'you know that?' said Charlie.

'Can't help it,' grinned Filly. 'She's amazing.'

Charlie gazed across the dance floor. 'I know,' he muttered, but he wasn't talking about Rihanna.

Charlie took a big breath and stepped onto the dance floor. Ant had moved into dodgy territory. He was dancing right behind the group that Rihanna, her team mates *and* Kelly were in. As Charlie bustled his way across the floor, he noticed Rihanna moving toward him. *What's she doing?* Charlie worried. He looked around toward Filly. Filly wasn't the tallest of the team, and he was jumping up and down trying to catch a glimpse of what was going on as there was now a group dancing in his line of vision. He looked like a little terrier hopping up and down on the spot, panicking that some other dog was about to run off with his bone.

Finally, Charlie reached Ant, but not before Rihanna and her friends reached him.

'Are you Charlie?' Rihanna cracked a big chewing gum bubble almost into Charlie's face.

Charlie leaned backward, tumbling into someone behind him.

Everyone laughed.

Charlie was mortified.

'Shut up! Don't be laughing at him,' growled Rihanna.

Suddenly, Ant snapped out of his dance trance and slid in beside Charlie.

'Yeah, he is,' smiled Ant. His face was like a tomato and he was gasping. 'I'm Ant.'

'I know who you are,' said Rihanna.

'D'you now?' smiled Ant. 'That must be me good reputation.'

'Yeah, right!' laughed Rihanna.

One of Ant's favourite tracks came on, and unexpectedly Ant joined in.

'Rihanna, it's your birthday,' Ant began to howl. 'Rihanna, it's your birthday.'

Ant started to roll his hips and do some mad funny twist with his arms, and his head was in sync with the rest of him as he sang along, throwing in some words of his own.

All the girls were hysterical, but Ant didn't care, in fact he was revelling in it. He loved the attention. Ant loved any attention.

'He thinks he's 50 Cent!' laughed Kelly.

'He's more like something from the two euro shop!' joked Rihanna.

Charlie was now tugging on Ant's sleeve to get him off the dance floor, 'Come on you muppet!'

'You going, already?' Rihanna was now dancing in front of Charlie.

Charlie rolled his eyes toward Kelly to catch a glimpse of her reaction. Kelly swiftly turned away so as not to make eye contact.

'Eh! Yeah,' trembled Charlie, and he looked around to check if Zucko was back from the toilets.

Zucko was standing beside Filly, who now had a clear view of the whole dance floor. Filly was in a state of shock, and it didn't help that Zucko was winding him up.

'Come on, Ant,' Charlie pleaded.

'In a minute' said Ant. 'Chillax man, the night's young.'

Charlie had enough. He was just about to leave the floor, when Rihanna dropped a bombshell.

'Kelly says you have some moves on ya.'

Charlie stopped in his tracks.

'Yeah, Charlie, do you have the moves like Jagger?' One of Rihanna's friends laughed.

'What?' shrieked Charlie.

'On the pitch!' Kelly added. 'I meant he's a good footballer.'

All of a sudden, Charlie felt that he had a reason to stay a little longer. Kelly was talking about him to her friends.

She must like me, Charlie thought.

'Makes no difference,' laughed Rihanna. 'If you have good moves on the pitch then you'll have good moves on the dance floor. Go on, show us your moves, superstar.'

Charlie went bright red.

'You're dead right, Rihanna,' said Ant.

'I know I am,' smiled Rihanna and she cracked another giant gum bubble. 'So you must be a crap footballer.'

Everyone laughed, including Charlie and Kelly. That joke had taken the heat off Charlie.

Ant didn't care. He just smiled at Rihanna and rolled his hips a bit faster.

Out of nowhere, Murph gate crashed the banter. He grabbed Kelly's arm and whispered something into her ear. Charlie noticed Kelly shaking her head.

Murph looked angry, and he leaned in to whisper in Kelly's ear again. Kelly pulled away.

'It's your turn!' Murph shouted.

'Shut up, will ya!' Kelly snapped and she checked to see who was watching them.

Kelly noticed Charlie looking over at them. She pushed Murph and stormed off the dance floor. Murph followed.

Charlie told Ant that he had to go, and why.

'Aw, I forgot about that,' Ant apologised. 'Sorry pal. Let me go to the toilet and we'll leave then.'

Charlie and Zucko waited near the door for Ant, not far from where Kelly and Murph were having a big argument.

'Look at them two' said Zucko. 'What's that all about, d'you think?'

Charlie shook his head. 'I'm going over. He's after pushing her.'

'Leave it man,' said Zucko, but Charlie didn't listen; he rushed over and grabbed Murph's arm, 'What's your problem?'

Murph pulled away and stared down Charlie. 'Get lost, Manchester, or I'll slap the head off ya.'

'Go on then!' fired Charlie.

Kelly jumped in between them. 'Will yiz stop?' She pushed Murph away from Charlie.

'I'm going, right? Now get lost, Terry's watching ya. You'll be kicked out.'

Murph brushed against Charlie's shoulder and disappeared back into the dance hall.

'Are you all right?' Charlie smiled at Kelly.

'Leave me alone, and mind your own business!' snapped Kelly and she left.

What was that for? Charlie was confused. *I thought she liked me.*

CHAPTER 16

OVER THE HEDGE

e haven't a hope of getting in there,' said Zucko.

'We have to,' said Charlie.

'Yeah, but even if we do get in, we might not be able to get back out,' Ant added. 'I don't think I wanna go in there.'

'I *have* to get me granddad's ball back, so I'm going in,' argued Charlie. 'You two can wait out here if yiz want.'

'Nice one,' smiled Zucko.

'Yeah, we'll keep sketch,' said Ant.

Zucko pushed Ant's arm. 'Keep sketch for what? It's not like there's anyone around. No one comes into the Lair anymore.'

'You never know,' said Ant and he pushed Zucko back.

'Will yiz give it up?' Charlie snapped. 'This is serious!'

'It's more like an adventure,' said Zucko.

'No,' said Charlie. 'It's not an adventure. Adventures are something that you enjoy. This is not enjoyable.'

'Fair point,' said Zucko.

'How are you gonna get in?' asked Ant.

Charlie stood back from the hoarded gate. 'I'm going over the hedge.'

As Ant was a bit beefier than Zucko, he was nominated to give Charlie a hooch up and onto the top of the hedge. Zucko's job was to make sure Ant kept his balance and not let Charlie fall.

'Ah, you kicked me in the snot!' Ant cried as Charlie swung his leg up and onto Ant's shoulder.

Zucko was trying his best not to laugh, but he couldn't resist.

'Shut up, Zucko,' said Ant.

Now Charlie was giggling.

'Give it up, the pair of yiz,' warned Ant. 'I swear, Charlie, I'll let you drop.'

Charlie was now standing on both of Ant's shoulders and Ant was rocking from side to side.

'Will you stay easy, Ant!' said Zucko.

'Come on, what are you doing Charlie?' gasped Ant. 'You're killing me.'

'Stay easy!' said Charlie. 'I'm trying to get a good grip of the hedge.'

'It's too tall.'

Zucko was right. Charlie's waist was still below the top of the hedge.

'Zucko, you're gonna have to push me feet up and give me an extra shove,' said Charlie.

'Make it quick,' whined Ant. 'Me shoulders are breaking.'

Charlie lifted his heels and Zucko grasped the soles of his shoes.

'On three,' said Zucko. 'One – two – three.'

'Aaaaaaaargh.' Charlie shot over the hedge and landed in a cluster of thistles on the other side.

'You all right, Charlie?' Zucko called out.

There was no answer.

'We killed him!' said Ant.

'Don't be thick!' Zucko chuckled. 'Charlie!'

'Aw, no way!' Charlie replied.

'What?' asked Ant.

'I think I landed in dog crap!' cried Charlie.

Zucko and Ant burst out laughing.

'Wait!' gasped Ant. 'Is the dog out?'

'No,' said Charlie. 'He must be in, and I can see a light around the side of the house.'

'Any sign of the ball?' asked Ant as he peeped in through a hole in the hoarding.

'It's pitch dark' said Charlie.

'Use the torch on your phone, Charlie' said Zucko.

'I am' said Charlie. 'I'm going over toward the house. It might be over there – back in a minute.'

Ant leaned back from the hoarding and looked at Zucko.

'How is he going to get back out?'

Zucko shook his shoulders. 'Beats me.'

Charlie looked everywhere for his granddad's ball, but there was no sign of it.

The old man must have taken it inside, Charlie thought as he stood in front of the hall door.

Zucko and Ant had got bored waiting so they decided it would be good crack to have a game of cross bars on the Lair, throwing stones at the goal posts.

Every now and then, Charlie could hear a *CLANK* coming from the Lair.

What's them two up to? Charlie thought. *That's it! I'm gonna have to knock on the door.*

Charlie stood in front of the door with his hand on the knocker for what seemed to be an eternity. His stomach was in knots, worrying about whom or even what would open the door if he knocked on it.

Just as Charlie had plucked up the courage to finally knock on the door, he heard chains being opened and the door handle began to twist.

Charlie stepped back onto the grassy path, away from the door. He lowered his mobile phone down so he was now standing in complete darkness.

The door opened and Charlie in all his wildest dreams would never have imagined what or whom was about to appear in front of him.

'It's you!' Charlie gasped.

Suddenly the door slammed closed. Charlie stepped back up in front of the door and lightly knocked on it three times. There was no answer.

'Please open the door. I can explain. I'm sorry if I scared you!' Charlie pleaded with his face pressed against the old flaky door. He heard the dog barking,

'Go away. What are you doing here? Get lost!' said a voice from behind the door.

'I'm sorry. I can explain. My ball, I mean my granddad's ball was in the garden. We kicked it over by accident the other day and I need it back, but I can't find it.'

There was silence for a moment. Charlie was giving up hope.

Finally, the door handle once again began to twist and as Charlie stepped back, the door slowly opened.

'You better keep this to yourself or you're dead.'

Charlie nodded.

'I will, honestly. D'you have me ball? Please, Kelly, I need it back.'

Kelly opened the door wider. 'You better come in.'

'What about the dog?' worried Charlie.

'He's out the back now,' said Kelly.

Charlie didn't know what to say next or even what to expect next.

How come Kelly lives here in this dump? He thought. *This is mental.*

Kelly told Charlie to wait in the hall while she went to get his granddad's ball, but when she came back, she was empty handed.

'I thought you had it.' Charlie was confused.

'Look,' said Kelly. 'First of all, I don't live here, all right?'

'But what are you doing here then?'

'This is me granddad's house,' said Kelly.

'Your granddad!' echoed Charlie. 'I don't understand.'

'What's not to understand?' Kelly raised her hands.

'But like it's ... it's ... Charlie couldn't finish his sentence.

'Yeah, it's a kip. I know,' said Kelly.

'I didn't say that,' Charlie's brows went up.

'It's what you were thinking. I'm not stupid,' said Kelly.

'Sorry,' apologised Charlie. 'Do you look after him?'

'Sort of,' said Kelly. 'It's why we moved to Ballydermot last year. Granddad was getting too difficult for the home helps and he had the place all locked up and no one could get in.'

'I know that. I had to come over the hedge,' Charlie laughed.

'It's not funny,' Kelly snapped.

'Sorry,' said Charlie. 'Go on, I'm listening.'

Kelly continued. 'Anyway, my ma tried to persuade Granddad to move out of here, like, no one else lives here, but he wouldn't, so we had to move into the area nearby. Me ma does most of the looking after him, but me and Jake drop in too to make sure he's all right. It was my turn tonight.'

'That's what you and Jake were arguing about' said Charlie.

Kelly nodded. 'Sorry for snapping your head off back at the club.'

'That's all right, I understand,' smiled Charlie.

Suddenly they were interrupted by a voice from another room.

'Who's there? Kelly, who are you talking to? I don't want

anyone in my house. I've told you and your brother that. Is it Jake? Tell him I want him.'

'Is that your granddad?' Charlie asked.

Kelly nodded. 'You better go.'

'What about me ball?'

'Get another ball!' Kelly insisted.

'I can't get another ball!' cried Charlie. 'You don't understand. This ball is special. It belonged to me granddad and I have to have it back.'

Kelly shook her head. 'Well you better come in and meet *my* granddad then 'cos he thinks it's his ball. But be warned, he's a bit feisty.'

Stepping into Kelly's granddad's living room was like being transported back in time. It was very old fashioned and Charlie could feel dust hitting the back of his throat with every breath.

Charlie had barely taken two maybe three steps into the room when he was hit with a barrage of questions from Kelly's granddad.

'Who are you? What are you doing in my house? What d'you want? Kelly, get him out of here.'

'Relax, Granddad,' said Kelly. He's my friend off my football team.'

'Oh!' said the old man as he relaxed back into his armchair. 'What's he doing here? You know I don't like strangers near my property.'

Charlie noticed his granddad's ball resting on a sideboard next to where Kelly's granddad was sitting.

'I need my ball back, if that's okay?' Charlie blurted without really thinking of what reaction it might trigger.

Kelly's granddad looked left, and then returned his eyes to Charlie. Charlie sensed from the old man's stare-down that this was not going to be an easy task.

'What ball?' asked the old man.

'Granddad,' Kelly nodded toward the ball beside him.

'That's *my* ball,' her granddad snapped.

'No it's not,' Charlie argued.

'Get out, you little shite, ya,' growled Kelly's granddad.

'I'm not going without me granddad's ball!' Charlie insisted.

Kelly's granddad leaned over and grabbed the football.

'Your granddad's ball – who is your granddad?'

'Tommy Stubbs,' said Charlie. 'And that's his ball.'

The old man looked over toward a picture frame hanging over the fireplace.

'Tommy Stubbs. I haven't heard that name in donkey's years.'

Charlie walked over to the fireplace to have a closer look at the picture. It was the same one that he had seen in his granddad's secret room in the back of the shop.

'That's him there,' Charlie pointed.

'I know that,' said Kelly's granddad.

Kelly stood beside Charlie. 'That's my granddad there, in the other team.'

Charlie looked at Kelly. 'They played against each other in the

Legends' final.'

'That's right,' said Kelly's granddad.

Charlie turned to face the old man. 'Why won't you give me back the ball?'

Kelly's granddad clung onto the ball as if his life depended on it.

'This ball is rightfully mine, not your granddad's. It should never have gone to him.'

'You're him!' Charlie said slowly, thinking back to the story that old Paddy had shared with him. 'You scored a hat-trick in that final too, didn't you?'

'A hat-trick?' Kelly echoed.

Kelly's granddad said nothing at first. He just held onto the ball tightly with both hands.

'I know the story,' said Charlie. He turned to face Kelly. 'My granddad scored a hat-trick in that final, Kelly, but he wasn't the only one. The match finished 5-3 to Ballyorchard and Granddad was man of the match and given the match ball for scoring a hat-trick, but there was another hat-trick scored by a player off the Rosco team and he felt that *he* should have been given the match ball.'

Charlie turned and nodded toward Kelly's granddad.

'No way!' gasped Kelly. 'Is this true, Granddad? You never mentioned this in any of your football stories.'

Kelly's granddad rolled the ball over in his hands, examining every stitch.

'Your granddad looked after it well. And he got it signed by

Charlton. By God, fair play to him, minding it for me, and now it's finally found its way home to where it really belongs.'

'You can't keep it!' Charlie blurted.

'You can tell your granddad that he's had his time and now it's mine. The ball stays here.'

Kelly's head dropped.

'I can't,' said Charlie, his voice trembling. 'My granddad is dead.'

'Oh,' the old man sighed. 'Jaysis! I never thought Tommy Stubbs would go before me. He was a powerhouse of a man. Ah well, he won't be needing the ball back so. It's definitely mine now.'

'Granddad!' Kelly snapped. 'That's not nice.'

'I'm only saying,' smiled her granddad.

Charlie knew that he was not going to get the ball and hell would freeze over before Kelly's granddad would remotely feel sorry for him and hand it over. He was a stubborn old man who had a grudge against his granddad for almost fifty years and nothing would change the way he felt, but Charlie had an idea. He had noticed a pile of betting slips on the sideboard.

He's a bit of a gambler. Maybe if I challenge him to a bet, he might not be able to resist Charlie thought. *He seems the competitive type. I'd say he'd find it hard to resist a contest or even a re-match.*

'Okay,' smiled Charlie. 'I understand.'

'Good man,' smiled Kelly's granddad. 'I'm glad you've seen sense. Don't worry, kiddo, I'll look after it. I'll put it over there beside my trophies.'

'Are you sure?' Kelly asked Charlie.

'Don't worry, Kelly. It's fine,' said Charlie and he turned to leave the room. Just as he got to the sitting room door, Charlie turned around. 'It's a shame though.'

'What's that?' asked the old man.

'It's a shame that, that ball, that legendary football will never be a part of another match on the Legends' Lair, that's all.'

'What do you mean?' Charlie had the old man's attention. He was hooked and now it was time to reel him in.

'Ah, no I'm just saying that, em, like, eh, I plan on organising one more match on the Lair, you know like, a fiftieth-anniversary match to celebrate and honour all the players that took part in that legendary match – the one in that photo on your wall.'

Kelly's granddad sat bolt upright in his chair. Kelly looked at Charlie and knew what he was up to, and she liked it. It was clever and although she adored her stubborn old granddad, she felt that him keeping the football was wrong.

'What? When's this happening?' asked the old man.

'Very soon,' smiled Charlie. 'I just have to sort out a few things and as soon as the pitch is tidied up and that, it'll be kicking off.'

Kelly jumped into the conversation. 'What teams are playing?'

'Well, I was thinking that I was going to put together a team made up of our Ballyorchard team and as it's an anniversary match for the one fifty years ago, we could play against a Rosco selection.'

Kelly's granddad laughed out loud. 'Jake plays for them. Great idea kiddo – they'll hammer yiz though. Jake's always filling me in on their form. Tell me, are yiz taking bets on it?'

Those were the magic words that Charlie was waiting for.

'Ah, I don't think so' said Charlie. 'Like, money and that and gambling, it wouldn't be allowed. We're only twelve, like.'

'Shame,' Kelly's granddad dropped his head.

'Well, if it's just a bet you're after, we don't have to bet for money,' said Charlie.

'What do you mean?'

'Well, we could play for that ball if you like?'

'My ball – no way.'

'Fair enough,' said Charlie. 'I thought you said Rosco would hammer us, but obviously they're not as good as you thought if you're afraid to bet on them.'

Charlie walked out the door and waited in the hall for Kelly. He could hear Kelly and her granddad talking, but he couldn't make out what they were saying. After a couple of minutes, Kelly called him back in.

Kelly had the ball in her hands. Charlie thought she was about to give it back to him.

'Granddad's agreed,' Kelly smiled.

The old man was slumped back in his armchair. He had a face on him like a bulldog chewing a wasp. He wasn't happy with the situation, but Charlie had read him well – he was a sucker for a bet.

'The bets on so!' smiled Charlie.

'Granddad?' Kelly nodded over to the corner.

'Agreed!' snapped the old man.

'I'll hold onto the ball,' said Charlie.

'Em, the ball stays here,' said Kelly. That's one of the conditions.'

'One?' echoed Charlie

'Yeah,' said Kelly. 'The other is that I play for Rosco in the match.'

Kelly's granddad clapped his hands. 'You'll never beat the Rosco, not with both my grandchildren playing.'

'Agreed?' asked Kelly.

Charlie was in a real difficult situation here. He needed the ball back now, so his dad wouldn't find out, but if he didn't agree to the terms of the bet then he would look bad in Kelly's eyes and he didn't want that either.

Kelly's granddad extended his hand, 'Do we have a bet?'

Charlie looked to Kelly. She nodded toward her granddad.

Charlie walked over to the old man and shook his hand. The old man jumped up out of the armchair and clapped his hands. 'Nice one – bring it on. Let me know now won't you when the match is on. Aw, Jaysis it'll be great to see football out on the Lair again. I'm off to bed. Lock up Kelly when you're going and don't forget to lock the gate on the way out, there was a few scallywags out there the other day kicking a ball around.'

Kelly locked up and opened the front gate to let Charlie out of the garden. Zucko and Ant were still messing around on the Lair.

'You know it's going to be impossible to keep your secret about your granddad living here,' said Charlie.

'I know,' said Kelly. 'Don't mind what I said earlier. It's probably for the best anyway. Granddad can't go on living like this and it's a struggle for us too.'

'Come on then' smiled Charlie. 'We'll let these muppets in on what's going on. I have to get home quick then. Me da will be looking for me.'

CHAPTER 17

TIME TO TELL

Charlie spent the whole day on Sunday worrying about how and when he was going to tell his dad about granddad's football. Yes, Charlie and his dad were close, tight, *The Super Glue Two,* but Charlie didn't want to upset his dad. His dad had asked – insisted – that he keep out of the Lair and Charlie had broken his trust, and to top it off, lost Granddad's ball to old man Murphy.

Zucko and Ant tried their best to spur Charlie to come out with the truth, on the way home from school, the next day.

'Just tell him,' said Ant. 'Your da is sound, pal. He won't freak out or anything.'

'I know,' nodded Charlie. 'It's not that, it's just like, I don't lie to me da and I don't want to upset him.'

'There's nothing wrong with telling your ma and da porky pies!' chuckled Zucko.

Charlie and Ant looked at Zucko.

'What?' smiled Zucko. 'Everybody can't be telling everybody the truth all the time. We'd all be killing each other, wouldn't we? And then nothing'd ever be done or achieved.'

'Thanks for that, Zucko,' said Charlie. 'You're a real philosopher, d'you know that.'

'I do me best,' grinned Zucko.

As the three pals sat on a wall across the road from Charlie's dad's shop, Charlie took a big breath, 'Wish me luck lads.'

Charlie slid off the wall, but just as he was crossing the road, he noticed Kelly and her brother coming out of the shop. They were fighting again, only this time it wasn't about their granddad.

'Here he is now,' sneered Murph as he nodded in Charlie's direction.

Zucko and Ant hopped off the wall to back their pal up.

'Leave him alone, Murph,' Zucko warned.

'Shut up you, you dope,' growled Murph.

Charlie turned around to his pals. 'I'm all right – leave it.'

'We have your back, Charlie,' smiled Ant.

Charlie nodded in appreciation and turned back to face his adversary.

'What did you mean, *here he is now*?' Charlie quizzed Murph.

Kelly went bright red. 'Don't mind him, Charlie. He's a thick. I'm after sticking up for ya.'

'What?' Charlie was confused.

Murph started laughing.

'What are you laughing at, you muppet?' Zucko snapped. He

hated Murph and he was getting really wound up.

Charlie stepped right up to Murph's face. 'What's so funny?'

Murph leaned in to Charlie. Their foreheads were almost touching.

'He's trying to snog you, Charlie!' said Zucko.

'Shut up, Zucko,' Ant elbowed Zucko in the ribs.

Even Zucko's humour didn't distract Charlie and Murph's intense confrontation.

'I said, *What's so funny*?' Charlie repeated.

'You!' snarled Murph.

Kelly reached in and grabbed her brother's arm to pull him away from Charlie.

Murph lashed out and Kelly fell back. For the first time in his life, Charlie Stubbs saw red. He grabbed Murph and pushed him back against the bin outside his granddad's shop.

'Go on, Charlie,' cheered Zucko. 'Slap the head off him.'

'Shut up, Zucko,' Ant didn't want Charlie to get into any more trouble than he was already in.

Murph stumbled to his feet and lunged his fists toward Charlie, but the superstar footballer sidestepped and stuck his right foot out, sending Murph flying across the pavement.

'I'll kill ya!' roared Murph.

Unexpectedly, Charlie's dad ran out of the shop and stood between Murph and his son.

'On your bike!' warned Charlie's dad.

Murph grabbed his school bag and turned on his heels. 'I'll get you for this.'

Kelly walked over to Charlie. 'Sorry, Charlie. I tried to stop him. It had nothing to do with me.'

Charlie was confused. '*What* had nothing to do with you?'

'In the shop, son!' Charlie's dad said sternly.

'We'll catch you later, Charlie,' said Ant, and he and Zucko scuttled away.

Kelly left too.

Charlie's dad closed the shop door.

This can't be good, Charlie thought.

'What's up, Da?'

'Have you anything you want to tell me, son?' Charlie's dad raised his eyebrows.

'Eh! What was that all about with Murph and Kelly?' asked Charlie, trying to change the subject.

'They filled me in on something that I'd rather have heard from you,' said his dad.

'What?' asked Charlie.

Once again, Charlie's dad raised his eyebrows. 'Something about a football match on the Lair that you're planning.'

Charlie couldn't believe what he was hearing. Why would Kelly do that? She knew that Charlie still had to tell his dad about Granddad's football and about him being in the Lair when he was told not to go there.

'Sorry, Da,' Charlie dropped his head.

'I *told* you not to go there, didn't I, son?'

Charlie nodded.

'Then why did ya?'

''Cos I needed to see the Lair, Da. I had to see it for myself.'

'But I warned you not to go there, Charlie.'

'Why, Da? I don't understand. It's not dangerous like you said. I don't understand why you're so angry.'

'You broke my trust, son. That's what's important here – not whether the Lair is dangerous or not, but that I can trust you.'

'You can trust me, honestly, Da. I still don't understand what your problem is with the Lair.'

There was a pause of silence for a moment, before Charlie's dad answered his question. 'I knew about him.'

'What?' Charlie was confused. 'Knew about who?'

'Your man Murphy, the oul fella living in the Lair.'

'What? How? You never said anything to me. Did Granddad tell ya?'

Charlie's dad shook his head. 'No, son. I heard Paddy and Granddad's other pals talking about it when I had them in the shop that day. I asked Paddy not to mention it to you.'

Charlie thought for a moment. 'He was gonna tell me, I'm sure he was and then you came out of the shop, Da. I don't get it. Why did you not want me to know?'

'Because I knew it would lure you into the Lair, that's why and I also knew that you'd go looking for oul Murphy.'

'But why would I want to go looking for him? I don't understand.'

'Because you're a good kid and …' Suddenly Charlie's dad stopped speaking ... 'Look the point I'm trying to make is that I didn't want you going near that place and you did.'

'Sorry, Da,' Charlie's head dropped again. 'I suppose they told you everything, like about Granddad's football and all.'

Charlie's dad nodded. 'Your pal Murph filled me in on the whole story. Nice piece of work, he is.'

'He's not my pal!' said Charlie.

'I know that, son,' said dad. 'I was just being sarcastic.'

Charlie's dad headed toward the shop door.

'I better open up again. Mrs. Casey is after peeping in twice already. You know what she's like for gossiping.'

'Am I grounded, Da?' Asked Charlie.

Charlie's dad took a deep breath. 'I don't know, son. We'll see. I don't want to make too much of an issue here. I just want you to understand where I'm coming from, that's all.'

'Thanks,' smiled Charlie.

Charlie's dad flung a marshmallow at Charlie's head. 'Eh! I haven't made up my mind yet. You're not completely off the hook.'

'Okay!' laughed Charlie.

'So,' smiled dad. 'The only way we're gonna' get Granddad's ball back and up on that shelf is to win it back?'

'Yeah!' said Charlie. 'Kelly's granddad is a stubborn oul git!'

'Well then,' smiled Charlie's dad. 'We've got a hell of a job on our hands to even get a match organised on the Lair. There's gonna be obstacles to get over.'

'Like what?'

'Well, we don't even know where to get permission from firstly and even if we do, it's in a bad way. It's not gonna be easy, Charlie.'

Suddenly, Mrs Casey marched through the shop door. 'Are yiz' closed? Your door was locked. Is everything all right? Is there something wrong? An emergency like?'

Charlie and his dad started laughing. 'No, Mrs. Casey, everything's hunky dory' said Charlie's dad.

CHAPTER 18

UNITED

The next two weeks were the busiest two weeks of Charlie's life. Charlie and his dad had a monumental task of seeking permission to stage the anniversary match on the Lair.

It turned out that the banks had control of the land after the developer went bust, but luckily, the wife of one of the Ballyorchard coaches worked in that sector and after a few phone calls and a lot of pleading, permission was granted for the match to go ahead, once there was insurance in place.

Once the club committee had heard all about Charlie's plans and how it would be a fifty-year celebration of a local match, which had involved some of their true legends, they had no hesitation in extending their insurance for Charlie's select team for the Lair. Rosco were up for the challenge and they too got behind their team and provided insurance for their players.

Every day after school leading up to the match, Charlie and his pals would go to the Lair and clean it up. They swept the whole pitch and the council came in and filled some of the pot holes with fresh tarmacadam. Charlie even managed to get local shops involved. They were given paint for the goal posts and a local sports shop donated nets and corner flags.

It was all coming together nicely. Even old man Murphy had his hedges cut low and the hoarding removed from his gate so he could see everything that was going on outside.

The big match was set for Saturday 21 May; that was the date that Granddad's big match on the Lair was held, exactly fifty years before.

Charlie couldn't believe that it was all happening. It had all come together nicely. Everybody had united and worked hard to make this happen and that made Charlie very proud and very excited about the big match coming up.

The night before the match, Charlie texted around all his team mates to meet up on the Lair; Charlie wanted to show them something he had made up for the match.

Everyone turned up. Although the Lair was a seven-a-side pitch, it was a big pitch, sized for senior seven-a-sides, so Charlie and Murph had agreed for the first time, on one thing; they would play nine-a-side with three subs. Everyone on the Ballyorchard under 12's wanted to play and so it was the same scenario with the Rosco team, too, so it seemed fair to put out a bigger side on the day.

Ant, Zucko, Tobo, Griff, Davo, Lee, Filly, Seany, Nailer, Heno, Ali and Charlie, all sat in a circle in the centre of the Lair. Johnner was away at a premiership match and Kelly had to play for the Rosco.

It was the night before the big game and Charlie was buzzing.

'So, what's the big meeting for, Charlie?' asked Filly.

Charlie had a small plastic bag with him. He opened the bag and took out a handful of arm bands.

'What are they?' Asked Ali.

'They're bands!' said Davo.

'For what?' asked Lee.

Charlie flung a few of the bands around the team.

'Aw, respect, Charlie!' said Seany.

Nailer held his band up close. 'Legends' Lair – 50th anniversary – 21.5.1966— 21. 5.2016 Legends live on.'

'That's class, Charlie!' smiled Heno.

'Yeah, your granddad would be chuffed, Charlie,' smiled Tobo.

'We'll wear them tomorrow, lads,' said Charlie. 'Tomorrow we'll be legends just like my granddad.'

'Yeah, legends live on,' chuckled Zucko, raising his arm band in the air.

All the players did the same.

'Up the Ballyorchard,' cheered Griff.

'Up the Lair,' cheered Charlie.

'Up Ireland,' cheered Zucko.

Everyone looked at Zucko. 'What d'ya mean up Ireland?' asked Davo.

'Ireland!!' echoed Zucko. 'The Euros are only a few weeks away.'

'Aw, yeah!' smiled Davo.

'Let's concentrate on tomorrow's match boys and then we'll

start cheering for Ireland!' chuckled Charlie.

As the twelve pals bonded in their circle, Charlie noticed someone walking toward them. He lowered his head.

'Here's Kelly,' announced Ant. 'She's been in her granddad's house.'

'Aw, team tactics!' loudly joked Davo. 'Team tactics!'

Kelly smiled. 'Don't worry, I wouldn't listen to anything you lot would have to say anyway.'

'All right, Kelly,' smiled Zucko. 'You all set for a hammering tomorrow?'

'Ha, ha,' laughed Kelly. 'Don't be too sure about that Zucko.'

Nailer held his arm band up to show Kelly. 'Look what Charlie had made for the match. Class aren't they?'

Kelly had a good look. 'Beast!'

Charlie's head was still lowered. He pretended to be looking at his band.

'You should be dead proud, Charlie,' smiled Kelly. 'It's a pity I'm not playing for our team tomorrow. I wish I was.'

Charlie never raised his head, just muttered *thanks*. He was still angry with her over the incident with her brother at his dad's shop. Charlie felt that Kelly was partly to blame for his dad finding out about the Lair and Granddad's ball, before he had his chance to explain.

'You all right, Charlie?' Kelly knew he was angry with her.

Charlie just managed a simple nod.

'I better go,' said Kelly. 'See yiz tomorrow, all right?'

Everybody bid Kelly goodbye, except Charlie.

Ant was sitting next to Charlie. 'Here, What's the story with you and her?'

'Nothing,' snapped Charlie.

'All right, don't snap me head off.'

'Sorry,' said Charlie. 'She shouldn't have done that on me.'

'Done what?' Ant was confused.

'Remember, the shop and Da? I told ya. Her and Murph told my da about me being in the Lair and what happened to Granddad's ball.'

'There's no way Kelly said anything' said Ant. 'That would have been all Murph. I'd say she tried to stop him and that's why she was there.'

'D'you think so?' asked Charlie.

'Yeah, you big eejit!' laughed Ant. 'You better make up with her tomorrow. You weren't very nice to her there.'

'I know,' worried Charlie. 'I will.'

'Good,' smiled Ant. 'Now, come on, I'm not sitting here all night. I'm after seeing Kelly's granddad out at his gate a few times. He's a nut job.'

All twelve parted company and just as Charlie was leaving the Lair, he looked back one last time at the famous football pitch and noticed Kelly's granddad standing at his gate. He was holding Charlie's granddad's football and smiling.

Enjoy it while you can, thought Charlie. *I'll have that ball back tomorrow. You wait and see!*

CHAPTER 19

WINNER TAKES ALL

Charlie stood alone facing his granddad's picture on the wall of the shop. As Charlie's dad was going through a few things out back with a delivery man, Charlie let his mind drift, thinking back to what it must have been like, fifty years ago to this day on the Legends' Lair.

He thought about the crowds of people who must have lined the pitch three rows deep and kids sitting up on the canopies over the doorways of the houses around the famous, yet humble, tarmacadam arena.

Charlie imagined his granddad scoring his goals and the final whistle being blown and all the Ballyorchard Legends jumping up and down celebrating their magnificent victory.

'Right, that's that sorted,' said Charlie's dad, interrupting his son's thoughts.

Charlie jumped. 'Me heart!'

'Were you daydreaming again?'

'I was just thinking about Granddad and that picture. It must have been beast, Da.'

'Beast?' echoed Charlie's dad. 'Is that a new word?'

'Beast!' smiled Charlie. 'Deadly – brilliant – classic. You know what I mean.'

'I think so, son,' smiled his dad. 'So are you ready for the big match then?'

Charlie nodded.

'Come on then. I'm locking up the shop.'

'Seriously?' Charlie was astonished.

'Too right' said dad. 'Your mammy and your gran are going to the match and I'm not missing it. An hour or two won't do any harm. Come on, there'll be loads there already.'

Dad was right. There were crowds already gathering around the Lair. Word had got around Ballydermot that, once again, a football match would be played on the legendary pitch.

'It's jammers!' gasped Charlie.

'Unbelievable,' said his dad. 'I knew it would trigger interest, but not this much. It just shows you, son, what people in the area think of football and this pitch.'

Most of Charlie's team mates were on the pitch already, kicking a ball around. There were some Rosco players up the far end doing the same. The pitch was surrounded with roping, keeping the crowd back a good two metres from the sidelines. This was done by some of the coaches from the Ballyorchard club.

Terry and Don, Charlie's coaches, were standing inside the roping talking to two of the Rosco coaches. Charlie ran over to them.

'Ah, here he is now,' smiled Don. 'The man himself – all right, kiddo?' Don put his hand out for a high five.

Charlie smiled and nodded.

One of the Rosco coaches extended his hand to Charlie. 'Well done, son. It's a credit to ya, what you've achieved here. Your granddad would be very proud today.'

Charlie shook his hand. 'It wasn't just me. There were loads of us involved.'

'Any word on your trial with United yet, Charlie?' asked the other Rosco coach.

Charlie shook his head. 'Nah! I think my da is gonna get in touch with my old manager back in Manchester and see what the story is,' smiled Charlie.

'What time d'you want to kick off at, Charlie?' asked Terry.

'We'll go with two as planned, Terry,' said Charlie.

Terry looked at his watch. 'Grand, fifteen, twenty minutes so. The refs just arrived so I'll let him know for ya, okay?'

Charlie didn't answer Terry. He was distracted by something going on over at the far side of the pitch, near the half way line.

'Sorry, Terry,' Charlie apologised. 'Yeah, that's mint, cheers. I'll see you in a minute.'

Heno noticed Charlie and announced it to the others on the team.

'What's he doing?' asked Nailer.

'That's that oul fella we were telling yiz about,' said Ant.

'Yeah' added Zucko. 'That's Kelly's granddad – the mad one. Come on boys.'

The team ran over to see what was going on.

'Leave it there,' instructed old man Murphy. 'That's grand – perfect.'

Kelly's granddad had got some men to carry his old armchair out of his living room, across the road, through the gates of the Lair and onto the side of the pitch just outside the roping along the half way line.

Charlie was mesmerised.

'Now bring the table over,' yelled the old man.

Kelly and Murph carried a small coffee table and sat it down beside their granddad's chair. Old man Murphy placed the legendary football on the table.

'Wow! That's legend!' said Seany.

'Pure legend!' Tobo agreed.

'It's signed by Bobby Charlton,' said Charlie.

'Woah!' gasped Griff.

'How old is that football?' asked Ali.

'Fifty years,' smiled old man Murphy, with one hand placed on the ball.

'It must be worth a fortune,' said Nailer.

'I'd say it is,' said a voice from behind. It was Terry, their manager.

He was holding a tall silver cup.

Charlie and his team mates spun around. They were now joined by Murph, Kelly and the rest of the Rosco team.

'What's that?' asked Charlie. He knew nothing of a cup.

Terry handed the cup over for Charlie to see for himself. Charlie read the inscription on the bottom. 'Legends' Lair Champions 2016.'

'Nice one!' gasped Davo.

'I know this match has a sentimental purpose for you, Charlie, and you're playing to win back your granddad's ball.' Old man Murphy interrupted Terry with a cough and tightened his grip on the football. 'But, eh!' Terry continued. 'We all thought, all the coaches like, that it would be nice to have a cup for the winning team and sure maybe it won't be the last match on the Lair. It could be a perpetual trophy, what do you think?'

Charlie was chuffed. 'Thanks, Terry. That's a deadly idea.' Charlie turned around and raised the cup for his dad to see. His dad gave him a thumbs up.

'I'll put it on the table here beside the ball,' said Charlie.

'Yeah' laughed Murph. 'Do that Stubbs. Leave it there because you're not going home with either of them today.'

'Shut your trap, you big thick!' Zucko blurted.

'We'll see about that Murph,' said Charlie. 'Winner takes all.'

It took Terry, Don and the two Rosco coaches a few minutes

to calm down the exchange of words between both teams and when the referee realised what was going on, he had a few words to say, himself.

'Everyone line up along the half way line there,' said the ref.

All twenty-four footballers faced the referee with full attention.

'Right,' said the ref. 'I hear this is a special day. In fact, I *know* this is a special day. I used to play on the Lair when I was younger.'

The referee was interrupted by a chuckle from Zucko.

'Sorry!' said Zucko, biting his lower lip.

'This pitch is legendary,' continued the ref. 'Do yiz know that?' All twenty-four nodded. 'It's been years since a football match has been played on the Lair so you guys should not only feel very proud today, but also very lucky, 'cos you know, it's said that this pitch was where legends played and not only that, but it's also been said that this pitch is where legends are *made*, so you guys are making history here today. This is the fiftieth anniversary of one of the most legendary football matches ever played on the Lair, so I've only one thing to ask yiz …' Everyone's ears cocked. 'Are yiz ready to become legends?'

There was momentary silence until Charlie couldn't hold back any longer.

'You better believe it!!!' cheered Charlie.

'Come on Ballyorchard!' cheered Seany.

'Come on lads, we can do it!' cheered Ant.

'It's ours for the taking, boys!' growled Murph. 'Up the Rosco!'

'Okay then,' the ref calmed them down. 'Keep it clean, it's tarmac not grass so I don't want any heroics out there. Win or lose, you're all winners today, don't forget that. We'll get on with it so.'

CHAPTER 20

LEGENDS LIVE ON

The crowd had waited patiently and were more than pleased to see both teams take up positions. It was just turning two o'clock, exactly fifty years to the minute that Charlie's granddad waited for the referee's whistle; now it was Charlie's turn.

Both teams kitted out in their club gear. It was an almost identical lineout to the friendly match on the Lawns, only this time Kelly stood opposite Charlie in the centre circle.

She had tossed a coin earlier with Murph to see who would be captain for the Rosco and Kelly had won.

On the referee's instruction, Kelly and Charlie shook hands.

'Best of luck,' smiled Kelly.

'Thanks,' smiled Charlie. 'You too.'

Charlie glanced over to the Ballyorchard sideline. He saw his dad, his mum and gran, his coaches and lots of familiar faces and although his granddad wasn't there, Charlie imagined him standing tall and proud, clapping his hands and cheering him on as he always did.

This one's for you, Granddad! Charlie smiled.

'All set?' asked the ref.

Kelly nodded and rolled the ball to Charlie, 'You tip off.'

'What?' complained Murph.

Charlie nodded and looked to Tobo. 'Ready?'

'Bring it on!' smiled Tobo.

'Come on, Ballyorchard!' roared Zucko from the sideline. Ali and Griff joined in. They didn't mind starting on the line. They knew it was a roll on – roll off match and they were part of a team, and everyone would get their chance to shine on the Legends' Lair.

Charlie took one glance behind him to make sure everyone was in position and ready for tip off. With a nod and a pass from Tobo, Charlie stepped over the ball and passed it across to Nailer on the left side.

Nailer controlled the ball superbly with his left foot and moved inside his Rosco opposite number with ease. He took a quick look to his right and hit a long pass across the Lair into the path of Filly out on the right, switching play to the far side of the pitch. This caught the Rosco defence out. They thought Nailer was going to go on one of his usual runs up the left.

Filly took the ball down on his chest and just as he was about to pass it back to Tobo who had raced over to support him, Filly was caught in the back of the legs with a clattering kick from the

Rosco left back.

As Filly hit the ground, the referee blew hard on his whistle and signalled to the Ballyorchard line for help.

'Are you all right, Filly?' asked Don as he helped the Ballyorchard forward to his feet.

'I was hacked down!' complained Filly, rubbing the back of his left leg.

'Come on kid, let's see if you can walk on it,' said Don.

Filly was fine. 'I'm sound.'

Charlie rolled the ball under his right foot as he waited for the ref to finish his talk with the Rosco defender.

Charlie never wasted a second on a football pitch. He used all his time while waiting to plan his next move and how he would help his team to score from this free kick, just outside the box.

'Okay,' said the referee, signalling to Charlie that he could go ahead.

Charlie had already had a word with Tobo and Nailer, and even their centre half Seany. They had it all worked it. As Charlie gave a hand signal to Tobo, Tobo and Nailer made opposite runs into the box to get on the end of Charlie's free. Filly was making a nuisance of himself, leaning back into the Rosco centre half and pretending to jump for a header.

The Rosco box was chaotic with players from both teams moving back and forth, and side to side.

Suddenly, just as Charlie saw an opening, he passed the ball across the pitch, low and hard. Seany was hanging around the outside of the box, unmarked. As the ball reached Seany's left foot he hit an unmerciful low and hard shot right through the gap that Charlie had spotted.

SMASH!

Just as the ball rocketed through the defence like a bullet seeking its target, Filly clipped it with the heel of his left runner, changing its direction.

As the Rosco keeper was sent the wrong way, the ball hit the back of the net and the Ballyorchard sideline erupted in jubilation.

GOAL!

All the Ballyorchard players ran over to celebrate with Filly, but Charlie was quick to calm them down. He knew that teams were always at their most vulnerable just after they have scored.

'Come on, boys!!' yelled Nailer. 'Keep the heads straight. Come on!'

Murph had the ball at his feet. He had called Hallo in to the centre to tip off with him. Kelly was positioned behind them completing a perfect triangle.

'Lucky start, Stubbs!' growled Murph, staring down Charlie.

'That's enough!' warned the ref. 'Let your feet do the talking.'

Charlie stared Murph down. There was no way he was going to let him get to him and he was still angry with him for ratting him out to his dad.

The atmosphere was destined to heat up.

As Hallo tipped the ball to Murph, Kelly expected the ball to pass back to her, but it didn't. Murph used his strength to plough through both Tobo and Charlie, and he went on a solo straight for goal. Hallo and Kelly sprinted after their centre midfielder along with the Rosco two forwards but Murph had only one thing in mind and that was to go all the way and nobody was going to stop him.

Heno didn't charge in with a tackle, he watched the ball carefully at Murph's feet and the second he saw his chance he stepped in with a perfectly timed tackle. The ball ricocheted off the two footballers and found its way out to one of the Rosco forwards who knocked a quick pass across to Hallo.

On Kelly's call, Hallo stepped over the ball and Kelly controlled it with her right foot, guiding it around Tobo and hitting a curving pass into the box and onto the head of the other Rosco forward who had snuck in between Davo and Seany.

Davo managed to get his body in the way putting off the Rosco forward but he still got his head on the end of Kelly's pass.

Lee's reaction was like lightning as he palmed the ball over the goal for a corner.

Now the Rosco sideline had come alive as they spurred their team on.

Hallo ran over to take the corner. His left back ran up for a short one, but Nailer had spotted this and marked him out.

Hallo knocked in a fast ball which somehow made its way through everyone in the box and found its way to Murph who was lurking around the back. Murph lashed out and caught the ball on the volley, sending it into the top right corner of the net.

GOAL!

Rosco had equalised and as the Ballyorchard players stood in awe, Murph spurred his team mates, punching the air with his fist and yelling that the cup was theirs for the taking.

The next ten minutes was all about the passing game. Both teams strung together some magnificent passes and keepers on both ends of the pitch were kept busy.

Before the half-time whistle came, both team coaches had brought all three subs on and Zucko who was the last of the Ballyorchard players to come on, made an instant impression with just five minutes left to the half-time break.

Zucko was a left-footer and although he wasn't the fasted player on the team, Zucko had the ability to tear defences apart, mingling his way in around tackles with the ball stuck tight to his left foot.

Griff had received a pass out on the left of midfield from Charlie and played it to Zucko with the intention of a one-two, but Zucko dropped his left shoulder and turned around his marker leaving him mesmerised.

The Rosco centre half charged in to steal the ball off Zucko, but the Ballyorchard forward threw a shimmy to the right and stepped inside him, leaving him with a clear shot on goal. Just as Zucko was about to pull the trigger on his shot, the Rosco centre half turned and stretched out his leg , bringing Zucko down in the box.

'PENALTY!' cries came from the Ballyorchard sideline.

The referee blew hard on his whistle as Zucko rolled around

the tarmacadam, holding his left knee.

There was chaos on the pitch as all the Ballyorchard and Rosco players tussled around the Rosco box, arguing about the tackle.

'You hacker!' Ali roared at the Rosco centre half.

'It's tarmac, you muppet!' yelled Ant.

Zucko was in agony. His left knee was badly cut and it was bleeding.

'We'll fix you up on the line, Zucko,' said Terry.

'I'm not going off,' cried Zucko.

'Your leg's in bits, Zucko,' said Griff.

'I'm taking the peno!' said Zucko.

'Let Charlie take it!' said Davo.

Zucko complained all the way over to the sideline. 'I'm all right. I want to take the peno.'

Charlie and Kelly followed to see if Zucko was okay.

'That was nasty,' said Kelly to Charlie.

'You're gonna get a few bumps and bruises playing on tarmac,' said Charlie.

'You want to watch yourself out here,' smiled Kelly. 'You have your trial coming up with United. You don't want to get injured.'

'True,' smiled Charlie. 'Good advice.'

Terry had Zucko's knee cleaned and bandaged.

'I'm going back on,' said Zucko.

Charlie had the ball in his hands. He threw it to Zucko.

'Are you sure, Charlie?' asked Don.

Zucko's face lit up. 'Beast!'

'We agreed!' said Charlie. 'Whoever wins a peno takes the peno.'

Zucko hobbled over to the penalty spot. He rolled the ball onto the spot with his right foot and took a few steps back.

There was silence all around the Lair as everyone waited to see if Zucko's left foot was up to the task of putting Ballyorchard ahead.

There was no run up. Zucko's knee was hurting him too much. The Ballyorchard striker casually stepped up to the ball and hooked it into the right corner of the net.

GOAL!

Zucko turned around to face the Ballyorchard sideline.

'*Now* I'll go off!' he smiled.

As his team mates danced around Zucko, the referee blew his whistle for half time.

Terry and Don kept it simple with their half-time talk. This was not a league match. It was a special match to mark a special day. Words of encouragement and praise for heroic efforts is all the Ballyorchard players heard on their sideline.

The Rosco coaches tried the same approach over at their line, but old man Murphy kept interrupting them, telling the players how important it was for them not to lose this match, and even though he was asked to sit back down in his armchair, the old footballer wouldn't budge.

The second half started the way the first half finished, with a bad tackle, only this time it was Murph who was facing a yellow card from the referee. He had jumped for a header against Tobo in the centre of the pitch and led with his elbow. Poor Tobo caught it right in the left ear sending him crashing to the ground.

There were no complaints from Tobo. He was strong and level-headed and he rubbed his ear better and quickly placed the ball down for his free.

Charlie had been marked tightly by Kelly and Hallo, but he stepped up his game and was beginning to dominate all the play in the centre of the pitch.

Tobo called Charlie's name for a pass, but he had no intentions to give him the ball. Charlie was too heavily marked so Tobo switched play, passing the ball back to Seany, but the centre half wasn't expecting the pass back and Kelly had seen Tobo do this before in training. The Rosco midfielder pounced on the ball and knocked it beyond the Ballyorchard centre half out sprinting him. Both Davo and Heno had come inside to close her down but they hadn't a chance to reach her. She took one final glance at goal and released a venomous strike at goal.

SMASH!

Kelly nearly took the net down.

GOAL!

'UP THE ROSCO!'

The cheers were deafening along the Rosco sideline as Kelly had scored one of the sweetest goals ever seen on the Lair.

All the Ballyorchard players held their hands up to their heads.

'Come on!' Charlie encouraged. 'Heads up, boys.'

As Kelly jogged back to the centre of the pitch she made eye contact with Charlie. Charlie smiled and made a gesture to Kelly. 'Class!' he whispered.

Kelly smiled with relief at Charlie's reaction to her goal. It showed just how dignified he really was and how he would make a true professional in the game. Kelly was worried that because she was really a Ballyorchard player, scoring against them on such a big occasion would have a negative effect on her place in the team, but Charlie had put her mind at ease.

Thanks, Charlie, thought Kelly. *Respect!*

Although both teams battled to get the winning goal, neither were able to put the ball in the back of their opponent's nets again and the match finished two all. All the players gathered in the centre of the Lair, wondering what was going to happen next and how would they resolve the game.

'Extra time?' suggested one of the Rosco coaches.

Terry looked to Don and Don looked to Charlie.

'Charlie set the whole day up,' said Don.

Charlie shrugged his shoulders. He had never been in a position before where he as a player would get to decide the fate of a football match.

'Ask the ref,' smiled Charlie. 'He's the boss.'

The referee smiled and laughed. 'Good lad. I feel important now, thanks.' The referee had a momentary thought. 'Look, why don't we call it a draw and then leave it at that?' He waited for a response but none came from any of the coaches or the players. 'What d'yiz think?' he asked again.

Before anyone had a chance to answer, old man Murphy came charging through the players and positioned himself right smack in the centre of everyone.

'There'll be no draw. This match has to be decided. A bet is a bet.'

Don was just about to calm the old man down when Charlie intervened.

'I'm happy to call it a draw,' said Charlie.

'Then the ball is mine after all,' smiled the old man. 'Yiz can do what yiz' like with the cup.'

Kelly saw Charlie's head drop. 'What about a penalty shoot out?' she suggested.

Charlie's head lifted. Everyone's heads lifted.

'Fine with me!' smiled the ref.

After a few disgruntled mutters from old man Murphy, it was agreed; the fiftieth anniversary match would be decided on penalties.

Five players from each team volunteered to take a penalty. There was no pressure on anyone; some players just didn't want to take a peno and that was fine.

The crowd pushed up from both sidelines and gathered around the top goal for the shoot out.

Rosco won the toss to go first and Hallo stood up to take it.

SMASH!

GOAL!

Filly stepped forward with his bright new astro runners, to take

Ballyorchard's first peno.

SWISH!

GOAL!

One each; a great start.

The next two penos from each team were scored with ease, from both Rosco forwards and Ant and Heno.

Three each.

As the atmosphere in the Lair was electrifying, Kelly placed the ball on the penalty spot. She took one glance at the right side of the goal and SMACK!

GOAL!

4-3 to Rosco.

Nailer struck his shot toward the opposite corner, the ball nipping inside the post as the Rosco keeper tried to stretch his finger tips to it.

GOAL!

That just left two players to take penos, and Murph had decided that he wanted to be the one to score the last peno for his team.

The Rosco midfielder smiled across at Charlie and then to his granddad who was clinging onto the old football as if his life depended on it.

THUMP!

Lee fisted the high shot up onto the cross bar.

Murph was devastated. 'Aaaargh!' He cried out with his hands to his face. The Rosco supporters couldn't believe it, but it wasn't over yet. Ballyorchard had one more penalty to take.

All the Ballyorchard supporters cheered their team on, but they were matched with equal cheers from the Rosco supporters, cheering their goal keeper on.

Charlie Stubbs held the football in his hands as he stood over the penalty spot. He blanked out all the noise and distractions from around the pitch and looked over toward the Ballyorchard sideline, his eyes searching for his best friend, his dad. As dad smiled toward Charlie, he raised both hands and gave his son a big thumbs up. Suddenly Charlie remembered granddad doing the very same thing in Manchester, the last time he saw him and that filled his heart with happiness and warmth and peace. He felt that his granddad was with him at this moment on the Legends' Lair and he was cheering him on.

SWOOSH!

GOAL!

Ballyorchard were Legends' Lair champions 2016.

* * *

As Charlie's team mates lifted the cup in the centre of the Lair and the crowds of supporters began to disperse back to the four corners of Ballydermot, old man Murphy reluctantly handed back Granddad's football to Charlie.

'It's really mine, you know,' complained the old man.

'Granddad!' said Kelly.

'Fair enough, you won it fair and square. You can keep it,' said her granddad, his head lowered.

Charlie's dad whispered something in his ear.

'That's why you didn't want me near the Lair?' said Charlie.

His dad nodded. 'That's the bit Paddy didn't get to tell you, son.'

Charlie looked down at his granddad's football, and then he shifted his eyes toward the old man. 'Is it true that my granddad said after your match fifty years ago, that the only way you would get his ball was if he was dead, and it was all yours then?'

Old man Murphy's head lifted. 'It is, and I have witnesses to prove it. That's if they're still alive. He did say that, he did.'

Charlie dropped the old football down into the old man's hands.

Old man Murphy smiled.

'But you won it back!' said Kelly.

'It wasn't mine to win back in the first place,' smiled Charlie. 'Your granddad deserved that match ball just as much as my granddad did. My granddad had his time with it and now it's his.'

Kelly helped her granddad back to his house, the old ball tucked tightly under his arm.

'I'm very proud of you, son,' Charlie's dad smiled. 'I know how much you wanted to win back Granddad's ball.'

'It's sound, Da!' smiled Charlie. Anyway, I think that cup will look great up on the shelf in the shop.'

'Granddad will be chuffed, son,' said dad, his voice trembling.

Charlie patted his dad on the back to comfort him.

'Don't be upset, Da,' smiled Charlie. 'We're on the Legends' Lair, and here, legends really do live on.'

CHARLIE STUBBS' FAVOURITE FOOTBALL FACTS

It is believed that football originated in China around 476 BC. It was known as 'Cujù' and players had to kick a leather ball through a hole in a piece of cloth hung between two poles.

The largest football stadium in Europe is the Camp Nou where Barcelona play. It has a capacity of over 99,000.

In a 1938 World Cup semi-final, Italy's Guiseppe Meazza's shorts fell down as he was taking a penalty against Brazil. He pulled his shorts back up and scored his penalty.

The very first international football match was between Scotland and England in 1872. The result was 0-0.

More than 80 per cent of the world's footballs are made in Pakistan.

A total of twenty red cards were shown during a match between Sportivo Ameliano and General Caballero in Paraguay.

The oldest leather football in existence is 450 years old.

Brazilian football legend Pele is the only player to be part of three World Cup-winning teams.

The highest score in a professional football match was 149-nil. Madagascan team Stade Olympique scored their own goals as a form of protest to an unfair decision made by a referee in a previous game.

It's believed that 3.5 billion people are football fans.

CHARLIE STUBBS' TOP THREE FOOTBALL TIPS

BELIEVE

Charlie says, 'You've got to believe in yourself. Having confidence when playing football is beast, but you must believe in yourself first so your confidence will grow bigger and bigger. Remember to always keep your head up and believe in yourself.'

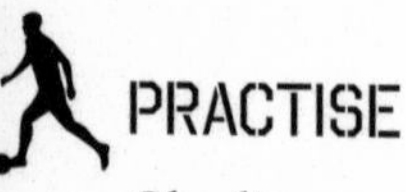

PRACTISE

Charlie says, 'They say practice makes perfect. Well, nobody is perfect and there's no such thing as a perfect footballer. We all make mistakes and that's sound. But if we practise we can improve. I always practise kicking my ball against the side wall of our house. Every second kick, I use my left foot. I used to only kick well with my right foot, but now I can kick well with both.'

HAVE FUN

Charlie says, 'I play football because I enjoy it. I don't play football because my parents want me to or because my friends want me to. I play football because it's fun and it makes me happy. Sometimes players can stop enjoying playing football for all sorts of reasons. If this happens to you and you are confused, try talking to your parents or even your coach. They're there to help you. Remember, the whole point in playing football is to *have fun!*'

WWW.JOEOBRIENAUTHOR.COM

www.obrien.ie